Queen
French Vacation

CW01637180

or
How To Politely Avoid A Man's Unwelcome Advances!

Andy Harris

Copyright © 2009 Andy Harris
All Rights Reserved

Cover image provided by London Borough of Richmond upon Thames Local Studies Collection

No part of this book may be reproduced in any form or by any electronic or mechanical means including information storage and retrieval systems, without permission in writing from the author.

ISBN: 978-1-4276-1121-5

Dedictated to:

The UK and US Military who

are doing so much for our

Nations at such personal cost.

With thanks to;

Niki, Sam, Bob and Geof for their

help and their copy reading skills.

Contents

Chapter 1

Her Majesty Queen Victoria was about to spend her 1882 vacation in Menton, the warmest and most Italianate of the Côte d'Azur/French Riviera resorts. Sir Henry Ponsonby, the Queen's private secretary, was deeply concerned over the security for the forthcoming journey and stay. Sir Henry's consternation was because the Royal Household had heard strong rumours (via the Queen's extensive Royal relatives), that Jeremiah O'Donovan Rossa, the Irish Fenian leader, was intent on kidnapping her Majesty.

As a result of this information, Sir Henry had approached the Home Office and they in their turn had tasked Scotland Yard. This is where we became involved. Let me introduce ourselves; I am Colonel Jocelyn Prendergast How would I describe myself? I am 6 feet 1 inch tall, very upright with a military bearing (not surprising since I have spent most of my adolescent and adult life in the military). I weigh about 13 stone (for our American friends that is about 190 lbs). People have described me as thin and wiry with fair skin and high cheeked angular face. I have a full head of fair-hair which has gone grey at the temples (if I was vain I would call it ash blond!). I have penetrating blue eyes (although when I look at them in the morning they look baggy and blood shot as far as I am concerned!)

My colleague is Superintendent Peter Smither. Peter is slightly shorter than I and a strikingly elegant figure always well turned out and somehow can remain clean even when chasing someone through a mud filled street. Some people would think him running to fat but in fact he is a bull of a man. I have seen him charge down three East End thugs and disarm them without even raising a sweat. Normally he has an unlit cigar in his mouth in an ivory holder. The uninformed would take this for an affectation but he has before now used the holder, which I happen to know, he designed himself as a weapon to disarm an axe-wielding stevedore.

We are both founding members of the Police Special Branch, which was initially created to deal with the Irish Terrorist threat.

I had been selected for my technical expertise in dealing with varied gentlemen from around the world who for some reason wished the Empire harm. I had gained my expertise in the military, serving the Queen in far-flung parts of the Empire. Peter had been chosen because he is the most outstanding and little heard of detective of his generation. It was he who mentored Sherlock Holmes in the art of detecting.

We were summoned to the Commissioners Office. This occupied a space on the top floor of Scotland Yard and over looked the magnificent Victoria and Albert Embankment, which contained the sewers that had finally controlled the cholera in the City. A favorite saying of the Commissioner was that it was a pity we could not devise a similar embankment to control crime.

The Commissioner is a short, balding, rotund officer of about 50 years old. He is full of nervous energy always fiddling with things or drumming his fingers on his desk.

"Superintenant, Colonel, please be seated," barked the Commissioner. "What are you working on at the moment?"

"The Russian spy case," I replied. "I think we are nearly at a point where we can catch the main people behind it."

"Drop it!" He ordered and then to Peter, "Superintendent?"

"The Fenian cell in Birmingham," Peter replied.

After a moment's thought the Commissioner stated, "Hand it over to Inspector Bottom or whatever his name is." (Surprisingly for a police officer he had a terrible memory for names and often would look blankly at a colleague until his assistant subtly prompted him.) I was convinced he wrote people's names on his blotter so that he could remind himself whom he was talking too. But could not confirm this since I could not quite see over his ink well which was in the shape of a "Bobbies" helmet.

"Do you mean Inspector Glutimus sir?" Peter asked, trying to suppress a smile.

"Yes that's the fellow! Just turn everything over to him. You two been asked for personally by the Home Secretary and on his orders, you have been attached to the Royal Household until further notice. You are to report to Sir Henry at Buckingham Palace at 2pm today. Smarten yourselves up and get over there straight away."

We looked at each other and indulged ourselves in a raised eyebrow apiece.

"Well get on with it," the Commissioner grumbled, annoyed to see us still sitting there.

We exited quickly but before we did, I managed to steal a quick glance at the Commissioner's blotter and saw there was a list of names with a line drawn through them. We were the last two on the list and he was just in the process of crossing us out.

Once we were outside the office, I turned to Peter. "I don't know quite what we are expected to do, but we had better not keep Sir Henry waiting!"

We both kept our dress uniforms at the Yard and, in the time, it took us to smarten up, a department carriage awaited at a side door. We soon arrived at another side entrance, this time at the Palace. (I seem destined to spend my life entering and departing buildings by either side doors or windows.) We were ushered up to Sir Henry's Office along richly carpeted corridors by a uniformed footman; the carpets absorbed the sound of our footsteps so somehow the building had a rather ghostly feel to it. The footman (who departed with out a sound or word) left us in Sir Henry's outer office.

We languished for half hour or so. There was little to hold our attention other than a large wall clock that ticked away the minutes. It had just chimed the half hour when the door opened and a group of harassed officials exited with armloads of papers.

Peter and I were ushered into Sir Henry's office. He was concluding some notes on the business of the previous meeting and for several moments did not look up. This gave us the opportunity to observe our new boss. He was a tall lean man, with a receding head of graying hair and a full beard. He was in his court dress uniform, so obviously he was prepared to be summoned to some official function.

Whilst we waited, I looked around the room. It very much reflected the character of Sir Henry. It was dominated by his mahogany campaign desk with it's neatly arranged in and out trays. It was notable that he did not use a pending tray. There was a large portrait of the Queen and the late Prince Albert on the wall behind the desk. The same wall held a bookcase full of military campaign books and weighty tomes on etiquette and the peerage. On top of the bookcase were two silver military figures.

A large afghan rug, of a deep brown colour, covered the floor. There was a silver framed picture on his desk depicting a family group with Sir Henry in the centre in full military uniform. He was wearing the GCB so it was probable that it was taken after his investiture. In front of the desk were two hardback chairs again of the campaign verity.

I knew that Sir Henry Frederick Ponsonby had the GCB (Grand Cross of the Order of the most honourable Military Order of the Bath, limited to only 36 knights and regarded as the highest Military honour) and was a member of the Privy Council. I also knew he was the son another British Army General, Sir Frederick Cavendish Ponsonby, who had fought at Waterloo. Sir Henry was an ex Grenadier Guards Officer and fought with distinction in the Crimean War and by the nature of his post he not only had to be exceptionally patient but also a master of protocol and a consulate diplomat.

"Colonel, Superintendent, please be seated." He ordered when he looked up. "What I am about to tell you is in strictest confidence and is not to be divulged outside this Office."

"Her Majesty will shortly be taking her vacation to the Rivera at a town called Menton and staying at the Hotel Chalet des Rosiers. She will be away in total for just under a month. It has come to our notice that the Fenians and in particular

Jeremiah O'Donovan Rossa are plotting to kidnap her Majesty and, we believe, demand the Kor I Noor diamond for her safe return. We believe the Fenians are in league with a splinter group of hard line Sikhs, lead by relatives of Duleep Singh.

Her Majesty is aware of these rumours, and refuses to be swayed from her plans. She also refuses to have any more security added to her household. As you know, the seventh attempt against her was just foiled on the 2nd March just over a week ago. She was shot at by a man, but a group of Eton School boys set about him with their umbrellas so preventing him pressing home his attack!

Anyway, after much pleading from the Prime Minister, we have managed to get her Majesty to agree to allow both of you to be added to her household. She graciously states you don't have to carry umbrellas'" Sir Henry looked up with almost a grin on his face but this soon passed and he continued. "You are to ensure that nothing happens to her Majesty and that she is not inconvenienced with any additional security measures. Is that clear?" We nodded in agreement. After a pause he continued,

"I am authorized to give you these. I think that is all for now. Thank you." With that, he passed a Royal Warrant across the table authorizing us carte blanche in the name of Her Majesty and a letter from the Prime Minister fully endorsing the Royal Warrant.

Before we could ask any questions, we were ushered out of Sir Henry's Office. We were informed by his secretary that we had been allocated an office in the cellars and the details of the forthcoming visit would be made available to us shortly.

We were led down to the cellars and shown our "office". By the look of it our "office" was a disused butler's pantry. As a precaution, I had a careful look around just to ensure the butler was not dead in one of the cupboards! At least the room had a window and enough space for about four desks that were notable by their absence! Clearly, the room had not been used for some time if the dust that covered everything and the rather damp musty smell were anything to go by. It was a damp and gloomy space and rather reminded me of a prison cell. There was a small fireplace and in the grate was a dead pigeon, which must have fallen down the chimney in the last 10 years or so!

I hoped this did not foretell the future if we failed in our task! We stood viewing our new domain each lost in thoughts.

"What do you think?" Peter asked.

"I was just wondering if I could get a fast steamer to Hong Kong and lose myself in the new territories!" I replied.

"I was thinking along the same lines." Peter replied, "Although I was leaning toward Ireland!"

"Well there is no way we are going to get out of this, and if we fail the consequences are unspeakable." I said and continued, "I've just read this Warrant. It commands all subjects of her Majesty to give us unquestioningly and immediately whatever we require and makes clear that the Treasury will meet any expense. (Knowing the Treasury, they will require a full set of receipts and three competitive bids! I thought.) Since we have been given seemingly unlimited powers, let's start using them! Firstly, we need a staff. Who can you trust?" I asked. "I can free up Sergeant O'Keefe. Granted he has one leg but he is the best "mister fix it" I know."

"I'll get Detective Sergeant Borne." Peter said. "We have worked together on the Irish situation. He has outstanding knowledge and experience of working on political situations."

"We need a telegram station set up here," I said. "O'Keefe can organize that and the office equipment. We have this afternoon to wind up our current projects, so we'll bring the Sergeant's up to date and meet them at 9am tomorrow. Lets get moving." I said hurrying towards the door.

The rest of the day was a blur of activity; briefing the Sergeants, giving them shopping and action assignments, which included a list of telegrams to send. All in all the entire list rivaled the activation list required to mobilize the household cavalry!

I finally crawled into bed at the Army and Navy Club at about 2am.Over the years I had been in the Special Branch I had found that the most practical home for me was a Club. Whilst I was serving in the Military, I had as a single Officer lived in varied Officers Mess's and before my wife's untimely death, we had lived in Regimental Quarters. However, on her death I had once again returned to the Club as a home. The Club worked well for me I had a valet and a suite permanently at my disposal. It had all the modern conveniences that London could provide including a massive claw foot bath with a shower arrangement that allowed three types of shower, Rainstorm, spray and torrent! The suite being situated at the rear of the building and near the fire escape it allowed me to come and go with out being noticed and allowed me an emergency egress should the occasion arise. I had taken the liberty on taking the room of fitting my own door made of African iron wood and a lock that would not only defeat the best picklocks in London but also withstand the attentions of crowbars and prizefighters trying to knock the door down.

However, even behind this door and lock, sleep was elusive. My head was a seething mass of questions, and the consequences of failure were weighing heavily upon me. I must have fallen asleep since I woke in a cold sweat at 5am having had a dream that we had failed to protect Her Majesty and were both for the "chop" at the Tower of London. I had woken up face down on my bed with my pillow under my chin like the executioners block at the tower. With a shudder, I arose and splashed cold water over my face in an attempt to clear my mind and achieve a more positive attitude on our forthcoming task. Walking to the Palace, I was surprised at the chill in the air and the layer of frost on the grass in the Park. It was cold even for a mid March morning, as the sun hadn't yet risen above the rooftops. If I was up at this time of the day it was normally me returning to the club after a nights work not as it was this morning getting up to go to work.

I was a pretty sad looking Colonel as I entered our new office and Peter looked even worse; tired and sporting a magnificent black eye and a nasty razor cut to his chin. He explained he had had to bring his pending investigation to completion before all the safety measures were in place. This had resulted in some of the suspects putting up a bit of a fight before being finally subdued.

The office had been completely transformed. There was a fire in the grate and the office had been cleaned and furnished with four desks and chairs, a filing cabinet, a black board, and a map of the world on one wall. The desks were fully equipped with stationary and I heard the familiar click of a telegraph key coming through the butlers pantry hatch. On looking in, I found a police constable at a telegraph terminal tapping away. He looked up on hearing me and gave a half smile in acknowledgement of my presence. I cocked an eyebrow to O'Keefe who simply said tea was on the way.

Sgt O'Keefe had served with me for more than 20 years originally from Glasgow. He was a short, lean individual; a product of the Glasgow slums. He had lost a leg in India while we were serving together and for some reason felt obliged to me since I had carried him some 20 miles while we were avoiding the attentions of some rather unpleasant mountain tribe men. He now sported a very fetching teak left leg, in which I knew he hid a bottle of whisky and a revolver.

Tea duly arrived and we all stood looking out of our basement window over the private gardens of Buckingham Palace. Its majestic lawns curving down to the lake. I was enraptured by the sheer beauty and peacefulness of the scene, and struck by the irony/incongruity of the violence and evil being planned against her Majesty. I drew a deep breath and said. "Right, let's get down to work!"

"How does Buckingham Palace know about this plot do you think, Peter?" I asked.

"The Queen has an amazing net work of correspondents so she must have heard it from one of her relatives." Peter said

"The first thing we need to do is get confirmation. Who do you know in America, Peter?" I asked. "Can we find out if Jeremiah O'Donovan Rossa is still about and if so who he has been seeing? I sent a telegraph to Brigadier Long last night in India to find out what the Sikhs are doing." Thank goodness the cable to India had been laid in the 1870's by Brunel's Great Eastern it made communication so much easier across the Empire.

"I did the same to Boston," Peter said.

"Good, What else?" I asked, and Peter continued.

"We need the detailed travel arrangements of Her Majesty from door to door and then the accommodation arrangements. We need to check all the staff, both household and those involved on the periphery: the people employed by the shipping, rail, carriage, and the hotel companies. We need to see if any have been recently employed, say in the last few months. We need to find out if any have Irish connections or sympathies, or Sikh sympathies and we need to check if any have had relatives disappear or are potential victims of blackmail." Peter stated.

"Then we need to check on Rossa and find out what he has been involved in. I know he was behind the bombings in London in the 70's. Then we need to do the same for the Sikhs." Peter concluded

"What else?" I asked again.

"Assuming Her Majesty heard about the plot when it was just taking shape, we can assume that the main suspects will have disappeared around that date. So let's check the shipping lines to see what ships sailed after that time to what ports and whether anyone answering their description was spotted on these ships."

"And we have to assume that we won't be successful in preventing the attempt from taking place. We must therefore prepare ourselves to guard the Queen. So let's put together a list of equipment we need and ensure we know how to use it." Peter said counting all these points off on his fingers.

"Well that should keep us busy for the next couple of months when does Her Majesty plan to depart?" I asked.

Sergeant O'Keefe looked up from a file he was going through. "Next Tuesday 14th March at 10:15am from Windsor Station, Colonel!"

There was a stunned silence followed by a rhythmic thumping noise. I looked across at Peter's desk to find him banking his head on it.

"Bugger!" I exclaimed, "How the hell do they expect us to do anything in a week!"

A tap on the butler's pantry hatch and a uniformed arm reaching through from the grandly named telegraph office interrupted us. (In fact an old china cupboard.) Sergeant Borne, a 6 foot 6 inch giant of a man who had played rugby for the Metropolitan Police Force and was their undefeated heavy weight boxing Champion reached over, took the proffered piece of paper, and quickly read it.

"Colonel, Superintendent," he said, "It's from Boston. Rossa disappeared over a month ago! Our man questioned the neighbours. They said shortly before Rossa left he had some visitors who had obviously been involved in some fighting because they all had bandaged heads."

"Sikhs!" We all exclaimed.

Our man also checked the shipping offices and found that SS Augusta Victoria had left New York for Europe at the time of Rossa's disappearance.

"Bloody Hell!" Peter muttered. "So he could already be in England or France, waiting for his chance to attack Her Majesty!"

"Peter, we need your expert knowledge" I said. "Do you know if Rossa had any associates in England that we could question?"

"How do you think I got this black eye? I have already set the wheels in motion and have a meeting this evening," he replied.

"We won't get an answer from India for some time, but Singh did have a house: Elveden Hall in Suffolk. Peter - can you try some of your colleagues to find out what he has been up to?" I asked.

"No problem." Peter replied. "Sergeant Borne, send a telegraph to Inspector June in Suffolk asking him for his assistance."

"Yes Sir," said Borne.

"Sergeant O'Keefe. You have the file in front of you. What is her Majesty's itinerary?" I asked

"Her Majesty will leave Windsor Castle by Coach with a troop of household cavalry as escort to the Windsor station. From there she will travel by Royal train to the coast at Portsmouth. The train will travel at 35mph," Sergeant O'Keefe explained.

"What!" I exclaimed. "35 mph."

"Yes Sir! There is a footnote to this effect. Her Majesty is insistent that it goes no faster ever since the Royal Surgeon fell off the train. Also she insists the train goes no faster than 25 miles an hour at night so that she can sleep undisturbed." Sergeant O'Keefe explained.

"Whose side is she on?" asked Peter.

O'Keefe continued. "At the channel she crosses by Royal Yacht Victoria and Albert, to France, escorted by Royal Naval torpedo boats." Once at Cherbourg the Royal party will remain on board for the night. The next morning there will be a reception on Cherbourg Pier. The Pier is not big enough for the Royal yacht to come along side so it will remain anchored in the middle of the harbour then Her Majesty will travel by steam picket to the pier. Then Her Majesty will travel the short distance to the City Train Station by horse drawn carriage and board her train, which will depart at 10am. From there she travels by her private train to the Riviera. The train is due to arrive at specially constructed station at the Hotel on the outskirts of Menton at 4.23pm on the 16th March. She will then transfer by private coach to the Hotel. HMS Inflexible will be in the harbour throughout her visit." Sergeant O'Keefe went on.

"Oh great! That will be a great help! We can order a 16 inch broadside if the Queen is approached by a stranger!" I said angrily.

O'Keefe looked at me and continued. "Her Majesty has a number of official functions whilst there which I have listed on the attached schedule. Naturally in the Hotel her standard security arrangements will be in force."

"Or lack of them!" I rejoined!

"Her Majesty is scheduled to leave for her journey back at 10am on the 12 April arriving Cherbourg at 6:30pm the following evening. Said O'Keefe.

The Royal Party will cross the channel on the 14th April. Arriving at 3.35 disembarking around 5pm. A train will then take her Majesty to Windsor. Where she should arrive at 7pm."

"I think we need more help in the form of a troop of men. What do you think Sergeant O'Keefe? Guardsmen or Lancers?" I asked

"Both Sir, if you ask me," he replied.

"True but we need to come up with a scheme to hide them from her Majesty - she does not want any more security staff around her!" I said.

"How on earth do you hide a troop of Guardsmen and Lancers from the person they are escorting?" Peter asked.

"You would be surprised, Peter. I think I know a way." I replied.

"Sergeant O'Keefe, use that Warrant and get me an interview this afternoon at Horse Guards." I said.

"Right Sir! Sergeant Keefe said leaving the office.

"Wait!" I shouted.

"Sir!" Sergeant O'Keefe shouted back, from down the hallway.

"Also, get me an appointment with the chairman of the Great Western Railway and our old friend Mr. Parsons the marine architect," I called. "I think he is staying at the Ritz."

Chapter 2

Sergeant O'Keefe had managed to secure me a 2 O'clock appointment with Brigadier General Pillsbury, late of the Life Guards. I arrived, as is customary within military circles, five minutes before my allocated time. I knew before I even arrived what was going to happen, and sadly I was not disappointed.

I was a Royal Engineer Officer before being elevated to Colonel. For some reason Engineers are generally held rather in contempt by the more fashionable Regiments. We are known as a rule as Mad, Married, or Methodist. To be honest, having observed my fellow Engineer officers, it does sum us up rather well. In peacetime, we are regarded as rather grubby tradesmen, but come war they can never get enough of us to help them out.

Since we were at peace, and I had asked for an interview at very short notice I was quite expecting the General to teach me some manners and my place in the great scheme of things. This he duly did by keeping me waiting for just over an hour. Finally, an orderly came and ushered me into the great man's office.

Whilst the office was as large as Sir Henry's it spoke of a completely different character of a man. The desk was in the centre of the room and had a row of trays along the front. There were several pending trays all of which were piled high. On the right of the desk was a silver salver with a half full port decanter and one glass.

On the back wall of the office between two large windows, overlooking Horse guards' parade ground was a picture depicting the charge of the Heavy Brigade at The Crimea.

General Pillsbury was a six-foot man resplendent in red tunic and side burns. A port soaked nose with broken blood vessels dominated his face. He appeared to be embracing the opportunity of being overweight and indulging himself at every occasion. Standing to his rear was a willowy Life Guards Captain who was holding a large pile of papers, which I assumed, were for the General's signature.

I marched up to the desk and gave my best salute. This was studiously ignored and the General continued to study some papers in front of him. I would not have been surprised if the papers had been upside down! I was tempted to lean over and set them on fire, but this whilst amusing to me, would not have helped the situation.

Finally, the General became bored of his play-acting, looked up, and barked, "Well I'm a busy man. Just what can be so important that I have to make time to see you?" He reached for his Port Glass which the aide quickly filled dropping the papers in his haste. This resulted in a tongue-lashing from the General and being told to get out of his, the General's sight.

Once the Aide had departed I said, "General please read this," passing to him the Royal Warrant.

He read it and his eyes began to bulge. "I do not believe this is genuine! I will have this travesty destroyed and you charged with insubordination!" He declared reaching for the hand bell on his desk.

"Before you do, General please examine the signature and Seal. You will see that it has been signed by her Majesty herself, and not one of her aids. Also please read this." I passed him an embossed envelope. I had been holding back with the letter. I had not wanted to floor the old goat but he had forced my hand. The letter was from the Prime Minister endorsing the Royal Warrant and further stating that if for some reason an individual or official withheld assistance to Superintendent Smither or myself, that person or persons would be judged guilty of treason and would be dealt with accordingly. He further stated that Superintendent Smither's or my word on the matter would be sufficient evidence of the commitment of the offence!"

It was an interesting few minutes. The General's face went from a port soaked complexion, via beetroot to deathly white. He also appeared to be having difficulty breathing.

Finally, he found his voice and this time the tone had changed to amazement.

"I have never in my whole military career seen two such unique documents" He said, "they make you and this,' he paused to look at the Warrant. " Smither, the two most powerful men in the Empire. What on earth is it all about?"

"I'm sorry sir I am under strict orders from her Majesty and the Prime Minister not to reveal the nature of our task. Suffice it say that if things went wrong the consequences would be catastrophic."

"General, I need to be released under my command with immediate effect a Platoon of Grenadier Guards and the Troop of Sikh Lancers that are currently visiting from India. They are to entrain for Windsor Castle within the next 12 hours and await my further orders. That is all sir. Thank you for your help. With that, I saluted turned to my right and marched out of the building.

My next appointment was with the chairman of the Great Western Railway. The appointment had been made for 5 O'clock on the assumption I would be delayed at Horse Guards'. I went by Department coach to the chairman's offices. Despite being early, I was immediately shown into his private suite of offices. These offices were reached via a large double mahogany door. Inside the office was laid out informally with a sofa and chairs grouped around a large fireplace with a painting over the mantel depicting one of Brunel's ill fated wide gauge trains. Behind the sofa was a large display case with a scale model of a modern Steam locomotive. On seeing me enter Sir Samuel arose from behind his desk where he was working and came towards me arm outstretched in greeting. He was framed by the large picture window, which afforded an unobcured view of the Great Western's main lines into London. From his desk, Sir Samuel could check the punctuality of all his services via a large station clock, which was hung above the door to the office.

"Colonel so nice to see you again, when was it we last met, two years ago?" He asked.

"Yes it must be!" I said. "Time does fly." Two years before I had been able to stop a plot to blow up the Menai Bridge whilst a train carrying the chairman was going across. For this reason, he seemed inordinately grateful to me!

"Sir Samuel, thank you for seeing me at such short notice. Would you mind reading this Sir?" I passed him the Warrant but not the letter.

"Good God Sir! I don't know what you have been tasked with this time, but what ever it is you have my and the Great Western Railway's full support." He declared.

"Thank you sir. I need two trains equipped to pull 60 men and 30 horses. They need to be pulled by your fastest and most advanced Compound locomotives. One must be at Windsor with the Royal Train in a week's time. The other needs to be waiting in France with the Queens Continental Train and will be required to go the south of France and remain on standby for about one month. During that time it must be ready at a moments notice." I told him.

Sir Samuel looked at me for a few moments then looked at the Warrant and looked at me again.

"Consider it done, and if there is any thing else we can do, do not hesitate for one moment to contact me directly. You have obviously been given a very heavy responsibility, but I can think of no one better to handle such a duty!" he said.

"Thank you Sir. You have my and Her Majesty's thanks." I replied. "There may be one further requirement. The train in France may have to carry a large piece of equipment."

"No problem you just give us the weight and the dimensions and we will do the rest!" he declared

"Thank you again sir!" I replied grasping his hand.

My next appointment was not until 8pm at the Ritz Hotel for dinner with Mr. Charles Parsons. I therefore returned to the Palace to bring the others up to date and find out if there had been any further activity or news. Peter greeted me like a long lost cousin.

"Thank goodness you came back in. I was just about to task Scotland Yard with finding you. I have a job for you tonight that involves your special skills." He declared.

I raised an eyebrow. "What's going on?"

"We need to enter premises tonight after dark and look at some papers that I believe are there. Last night we managed to get our hands on a Fenian activist who after a bit of persuasion told us about a building in the docklands that might hold a few clues as to the where abouts of Rossa and his cronies. Unfortunately, I don't have enough to convince a Magistrate to issue a search warrant. Even with our Royal Warrant. Also, I don't believe it would be in our interests to let it be known we know about the property. Do you have those special little tools of yours to hand?" Peter asked.

"You told me if a policeman ever caught me in possession of those I'd get 25 years hard labour!" I relied with a smile.

"Well as they say, how things change!" Peter said.

I explained I was meeting Mr. Parsons for dinner at eight, but should be able to make my excuses by eleven or so.

Peter said he would have a Department coach and a change of clothes meet me at that time at the hotel.

I looked at the office clock. Sergeant O'Keefe had somehow acquired a magnificent timepiece for us, which looked suspiciously like the one that had been in the anti room of Sir Henry's office. I believed that if I hurried, I could get back to my club, change for dinner, pick up my tools, and be on time at the hotel. I made my excuses and left at a brisk walk. I walked back to the club through Regents Park. It was now twilight and the lamplighters were busy lighting the gas lamps. My head was full of questions and doubts. Were we on the right track? what would tonight hold and were we up to the challenge?

I must have been totally preoccupied because it was only at the last minute I realized I was being followed and the individual was closing quickly behind me. I abruptly changed direction reversing my course and closing the gap between my pursuer and myself. He was a scruffy street thief who obviously had decided I was easy pray. As I approached him I slammed my open palm under his chin and forcing his head back, and swept his legs under him as he pulled a knife from his pocket.

He fell down to the ground and I pushed my knee into his chest and flicked the knife out of his reach. He was swearing and kicking but was unable to move. I pulled my police whistle from my pocket and blew until some police came to my aid. A young constable came running up and once I had showed him my police warrant card he cuffed the footpad and led him away.

Some how the incident had cleared my mind and the lingering doubts had gone. I checked my pocket watch and realized I needed to hurry if I was going to make my appointment.

I arrived at the hotel with about 5 minutes to spare. I gave my card to the front desk attendant who clearly was an old soldier by his stance and bearing. He snapped to attention on seeing my Military rank on my card and said he would take it personally. Whilst I was waiting, I looked around the lobby and the people gathered there. There were several swells and others in evening dress about to depart for the theatre. It wasn't long before Mr Charles Parsons came into the lobby, shook me by the hand, and led the way into the dining room. During an excellent dinner, of roast beef accompanied by an outstanding bottle of claret, I passed the Warrant across the table to Mr Parsons who barely looked at it.

"Colonel for what I owe you, you don't need to show me paperwork or justify anything, just ask and I will do what I can to help" He declared.

"That is very generous Mr. Parsons. I need to borrow your prototype boat sir. And I need to keep it for about a month in France." I stated.

"I won't ask how you knew the boat even existed, since it is my closest guarded secret but if you need her she is yours along with a handpicked and totally trustworthy crew. I assume it will be involved in the violence that you always somehow seem end up in, so if it's all the same to you I will add a couple of modifications to the vessel before I deliver her. Where and when do you need her?" Mr Parsons asked.

I explained that I needed her at the Port of Dover in a week's time, and then I would transport her by rail to the South of France. I told Mr Parsons that if he could outline his requirements for transport to Great Western Railways they would make the necessary arrangements for him.

The conversation moved on to reminiscing about our past experiences and the joint adventure we had shared just a few years before. This had culminated in my rescuing Mr. Parsons and ensuring his turbine designs were not stolen and sent abroad to another world power. Eleven o'clock came all too quickly; I made my excuses and promised (as far as it was within my power) not to do too much damage to his boat.

I picked up the leather bag I had deposited with the hotel and assured myself that it had not been interfered with. The average bag snatcher would have had his work cut out to open the locks or even cut through the leather, which was lined with chain mail.

I took a deep breath, and stepped outside and immediately saw Peter standing in the light of a gas street lamp across the road. Next to him stood a nondescript horse drawn four-wheeler. The horses waited patiently and absent-mindedly chewing in their nosebags. The evening had grown cold and I felt a shiver down my spine, though not entirely from the lack of warmth in the air. I had an odd feeling of foreboding, as I knew we would not be welcome visitors where we were going............

Chapter 3

As I crossed over the road to the carriage, I noticed that the driver was none other than Sergeant O'Keefe dressed as a rather disreputable coachman. He had a large blanket wrapped around him, which I somehow felt covered more than his body. The casual observer would conclude that the coach had seen better days and was held together by the woodworms holding hands. However if one looked further the first thing to be noticed was the horses whilst mud splattered where in fact in the prime of life well muscled and chaffing at the bit to be off. The harnesses undoubtedly were dirty but the leather was well oiled and proficiently coupled to the coach the running gear of which was heavily greased.

I jumped into the coach and was greeted by Sergeant Borne who had been to my club and brought a change of clothes for me. I stripped off in front of the others as O'Keefe got under way, every now and then having to grab one by the shoulder for support as the carriage went around a corner. I exchanged my dining attire for a grey working suit and rubber soled shoes.

Peter said looking at my bare back.

"If you carry on the way you have, you are going to run out of scar tissue."

I had to admit that my body appeared to be about half scar tissue and half skin! I laughed and replied that:

"I happen to know you are in the same state as me!"

He became serious "Right, then, this is the situation. You will recall I said I had carried out a raid yesterday. We have had a chance to question one of the suspects in depth. He is terrified not only of us but also of the Fenians. If they found out he had talked or even if he had been seen in our presence, he is a dead man. I have convinced him we can arrange for him to disappear, and as a result, he has told us of a warehouse in Docklands owned by a mysterious company. It looks like our only lead at the moment. I sent Sergeant Borne around, he reported that the building whilst new seems to be deserted, but the locks on the doors, and windows are state of the art. That's why I thought of you!"

Victoria docks were our destination. As we made out way through the grimy streets which grew narrower and darker, giving a foreboding feeling to the journey. I sat in the coach, opened my case, and reviewed my instruments. I pulled out the waistcoat with the specially lined pockets and started fitting the tools in their requite pockets. I then took out the shuttered lamp and checked the wick was clean. Finally, I took out my specially designed Sanderson camera and I fitted it into the small backpack along with the specially coated glass plates.

I leaned forward and spoke to O'Keefe through the hatch.

"Did you bring the other piece of equipment?"

"Yes Colonel." He replied.

"Great, I don't know if we can use it but one never knows and I have been dying to try it out." I said.

We arrived at the docks and Sergeant Borne disappeared into the night. It was a perfect night for breaking and entry no moon worth talking about and a thick river fog drifting in from the Thames. Sergeant Borne had bid me wait for his return and I sat in silence my hands checking the waistcoat was fastened and there were no rattles from its contents. I had lost count of how many times I had carried out similar acts but it never lost its thrill. I was looking out of the coach window at the building it had only just recently been completed and consisted of some four levels of red brick construction with large metal framed windows lining the river front and rear walls. The ground floor was recessed in the front and supported by robust iron Pillars. On the top floor there were posts sticking out at right angles to the building from which halyards were attached to be used to pull up sacks of produce. We sat in silence for a half an hour, or so and then there was a knock on the roof and Sergeant O'Keefe's head appeared through the hatch. "Sergeant Borne is calling you forward, Sir." He whispered. "Good luck."

I dismounted the carriage and keeping to the shadows moved towards the building. Sergeant Borne pointed out a side door and said the coast was clear. I moved to the door and looked at the lock. It was impressive but unlikely to cause a serious problem. However, before I even touched it I withdrew a small mirror from my waistcoat and pushed it under the door. Using it to reflect light from my unshuttered dark lamp, I looked at the inside of the door. I smirked, I spotted a wire connected to the rear of the door and running to a shotgun pointing at the door.

These people were serious. Keeping to the shadows, I moved around the building until I came to a vertical drainpipe to the roof. I carefully checked the pipe to ensure that it was fixed in place and not in any way tampered with. I quickly scaled the pipe to the first floor and stepped onto a windowsill. I cautiously looked into the window and after a few minutes dismissed it as a point of entry: more trip wires. I did the same on the second floor but it was not until I reached the third floor that I found a window that did not appear to be protected by trip wires and the like.

I removed a long spatula like knife from my waistcoat, slipped it between the sashes, and flicked the catch off. With great care, I then raised the window a couple of inches and pushed the mirror through the slit to check for anything untoward. There appeared to be no traps so I opened the window further and sat in a squat on the cold rough stone windowsill. I tried to ignore the chill germinating through the soles of my shoes as I studied my surroundings. There appeared to be no trip wires but considering this was not a flour warehouse there was a lot of flour just under the window. I concluded it was there to spot any footprints. I looked up and saw a beam over which I could flick a loop of rope and swing across the flour belt. Pulling a loop of rope from my waistcoat, I tossed it over the beam. In books, this is always achieved with ease at the first attempt but it took me three goes. During the second undertaking I nearly lost my balance and fell off the sill but I caught myself and after some choice muttered swearing, I succeeded in looping the rope over the beam.

Then only waiting to shut and relock the window, I grabbed both ends of the rope and merrily swung over the powder. I let go of one end of the rope, pulled it back off the beam, and stashed it back into my waistcoat.

After stowing the rope, I pulled a three-foot piece of 16-gauge wire from another pocket and fashioned it into what looked like a very deformed letter seven. The top stroke of which was very short. I balanced the wire by this stroke on my right forefinger and proceeded across the floor holding the wire in front of me dangling down to the floor. I had advanced about 20 feet when the wire tilted slightly at its bottom towards me. I hastily stopped and retreated half a step. I went down onto my knees and opening my dark lamp slightly so that I could see more clearly but at the same time not be observed from outside I examined the floor area in front of me. Strung across the floor about 6 inches above the floorboards was a thin black wire about the diameter of a human hair. I followed it to both its ends one was fixed to a screw in the outer walls skirting board where it was fixed via a spring to keep it tight. The other end was fixed via a rather complex looking arrangement to a shotgun, which was fixed in place and aimed along the wire's length. If the wire was broken or equally knocked, hence increasing the tension the gun would fire. Having noted the position of the wire I carefully stepped over it and again using my trip wire feeler advanced towards the stairs.

The stairs presented another problem. I used the trip wire feeler but examined each stair tread minutely before very gingerly putting any weight upon it. On the second flight of stairs, I came across a stair tread that looked slightly different to its fellows. And on examining it further, I noted that it was hinged at the junction with the one preceding it. I managed to step over it and on turning around to examine it further noted it was held in place by a very thin piece of dowel. Any normal footfall would have broken the dowel, which would have released the stair tread, which in turn would have acted as a trigger to release the whole flight of stairs. The stairs would have swung vertically so that anyone on the stairs would have fallen the remaining three levels into the cellars of the warehouse.

It took me another hour to work my way the ground floor. In the process, I found three more trip wires, all were connected to shot guns. On reaching the door that I had been originally inspected, I simply disconnected the wire to allow the door to be opened. It was wired to the gun via a wire and springs. There was a safety pin to neutralize the trap and attached to the safety pin was a small clockwork motor that when activated gave someone time to exit before pulling the pin out and activating the trap. Sergeant Borne and Peter were waiting in the shadows and when I opened the door, they quickly entered and I shut the door behind them.

"Who the hell owns this building?" I whispered

“Why?” Peter asked

“Because it is better protected than the Bank of England! You wouldn’t believe the booby traps in the building, and they’re designed to kill!” I said.

“It is owned by a company whose majority share owner is John Devoy and Devoy is the best friend of Jeremiah O’Donovan Rossa,” Peter said.

“Right, well, they apparently have something in this building that they are very keen not to share with anyone else.” I said. “I saw an office on the first floor. I think that is the place to start our search. Follow me, but careful this place is a death trap!”

Moving painstakingly in a single file I led the way to the door of the office. There were no more trip wires or loose boards on the way. On looking at the lock on the office door, I saw it was custom-made out of very soft brass. Very clever I thought! Any picklock, not being cautiously used, would leave telltail scratches. A further examination around the edge of the door resulted in my increased respect! Carefully tucked, into the door jam was a small piece of card. If the door was opened, the card would fall to the floor and the occupants of the building would know someone had entered. What was more impressive was that a human hair had been stuck on the other edge of the door. These people were paranoid. I marked the objects' locations.

I set to work with a special set of lockpicks, (coated with a thin layer of rubber, so that the lock would not be scratched). Having successfully picked the lock I slowly opened the door and again checked for trip wires. There were none. It appeared that, because we were in a frequently used office, the owners did not want to risk falling into their own traps.

The office was clean but spartanly furnished with a large roll top desk and chair. In front of the desk were a rug and two hardback chairs. The only other piece of furniture in the office was a large safe in the corner behind the desk and I recognized it as a "double key" Hobbs safe. There was a large window similar to the one I had climbed through but this one had iron bars on both the inside and outside of the glass. I turned to Peter and said I thought the safe would take about 20 minutes to open, and could he go and get the special box from Sergeant O'Keefe?

Peter nervously exited and we started on the safe. There was some light permeating through the window from the streetlights but not enough to see properly. I therefore used the piece of black silk I had brought for the purpose to black out the window and once I was satisfied no light could be seen from outside fully opened my lamp to give us full illumination of the task in hand. It was complex, but after 20 minutes of methodically trying and filing blank keys, I managed to unlock the door. The keys had a very light coating of carbon dust on their key faces so that when I pushed them into the locks and applied pressure the carbon was removed showing me where I had to file the keys down to fit. Once I was happy with both my new keys, I turned them in the locks and felt with satisfaction the mechanisms unlock. I grasped the lever that pulled the retaining bolts back within the door body but only after a painstaking check that there were no pieces of paper or hair as markers on the door did we swung it open. Inside, the paperwork and contents were obviously precisely positioned in a set order so that the owner would know if they had been moved. I could see we would have to be very thorough and replace everything in the exact same place.

We scanned through the contents of the safe and carefully selected the papers we felt were relevant, that is to say, were in some sort of code or simply had no relevance to a shipping company. We laid the documents on the floor and with the dark lamp fully illuminating the papers I started taking long exposure pictures with my plate camera. Since there were only 12 plates, we had to be selective as to what was included. It was at this moment in time that Sergeant Borne warned me someone was coming. We froze. I indicated that Sergeant Borne should take up position by the door and I behind the desk. I closed the dark lamp and drew from my pocket my leather cosh filled with lead. We crouched in silence ready to spring at whosoever entered the room. A figure approached and stood illuminated by the ambient light from outside in the door. He appeared to b carrying something.

"If you think I'm coming in there without announcing myself you have another thing coming!" whispered Peter.

As he entered the room and I opened my lamp, he informed us that dawn was not far off, so we had better get ready to depart. I methodically put the contents back in the safe in exactly the order they had come out and locked the safe door. I then went to the vent I had seen in the office wall and painstakingly unscrewed the grill and placed the box out of sight of the room in the ducting leading to the grill. I ensured that I had fully wound up the clockwork mechanism of the box. I replaced the grill and precisely aligned the screw heads as they had been and filled their screw grove with clear candle wax. We carefully exited the office, removing the silk from the window locking the door and replacing the hair and card. The card was simply held in place by the pressure of the door against the door jam. The hair was stuck in place by a judicial application of spit to my finger then running said finger along the hair. We warily stole from the building, shutting the door and ensuring the gun had recocked by simply winding up the little clockwork motor which slowly unwound pulling the safety pin out of the trip mechanism.

We then slowly drove away, keeping to the back streets with a sharp eye to ensure we were not followed. The streets in the dock yard were narrow and cobbled so that the horses hooves sounded unnaturally load particularly since the carriages harnesses were so constructed that they did not jingle and the wheels had rubber rather than steel rims so again did not make noise. In the past we had muffled the horses hooves as well with special leather boots but Peter had not thought it necessary on this occasion. Once certain we were in the clear, we headed for Scotland Yard arriving about 6 am.

We went to the Special Branch Offices and delivered our plates to the technicians who promised to develop them straight away. Sergeant O'Keefe reappeared to announce that breakfast was on for us all in the canteen if we would follow him. After hearty bacon, egg, kidney and kedgeree breakfast, washed down with a large mug of tea. Sergeant borne asked,

"What was in that box you hid in the ventilator shaft Colonel?"

"Oh sorry, I didn't have a chance to tell you. It is an adaptation of a phonograph with a very strong clockwork motor and slow moving cylinder. It has a diaphragm trigger, which will start it recording once someone begins to speak or makes a noise. Unfortunately being a prototype it cannot stop once it's activated, so we will only have the chance of one recording. And we'll have to go back into the office to get the device back and hear what was said. Sergeant Borne, can you arrange for the building to be watched so that we know when someone has been in the office?" I said.

"Consider it done, Colonel."

We finished our breakfast as the results of my camera work came in. It was amazing looking at the glass plates it was if the documents we had found last night were in front of us, but doubled in size. The majority of them were hard to read. In fact, they were impossible to read, since they were in code.

"Peter, any idea who we can get to decode these?" I asked.

"I think, the Foreign Office will be our best chance.' Peter replied. "Give me the photographs and also the Warrant. I will go and see what I can do. You go and get some sleep and I will see you at the Palace office at 2 pm."

"I will see you there!" I said. With that, I picked up my trusty tool case and headed for the door.

"You know, if you are ever short of money, half the criminals in London would pay handsomely for that bag!" Peter called after me. I turned, waved, and set off to the club for a well-earned sleep.

Chapter 4

I arrived at the Palace just before 2pm feeling much refreshed after a four-hour sleep and a very welcome hot bath to find a neatly piled stack of paper on my desk. Sergeant O'Keefe was clearly in the building, since there were more furnishings in the room. There was an impressive safe in the corner and a table that I was certain had not been there last night. On this, were laid the photographs I had taken last night.

I sat down to go through the paperwork. There was a telegraph from India, it stated they were contacting their man in the Punjab and would do their utmost to help, but it would take time to get an answer. There was a rather bitter letter from "Horse Guards" confirming details of the troop transfer and also one from The Great Western Railway and another from, Mr Parsons both asking if they could do more.

Sergeant O'Keefe came in the office with a tray; it contained tea and biscuits, which he placed at my elbow.

"Everything in order?" I asked O'Keefe.

"Yes sir, Sergeant Borne is down at the docks, with some of his under cover friends checking out the building you visited last night and Superintendent Smither should be here very shortly," O'Keefe replied.

I continued to plough through the paper work, making notes as I did so. The most urgent item that needed to be done was the housing and feeding of the troops who were on their way to Windsor. I made a note to this effect, on the pad of paper at my elbow

O'Keefe who was standing behind me, obviously reading my notes, he cleared his throat in a rather theatrical way,

"Yes Sergeant, what is it that you want to say?" I asked suppressing a smile.

Clearing his throat again O'Keefe began, "The troops have been housed and put on the ration strength of the Guard at Windsor Castle. Extra ammunition and fodder for the horses have been arranged. The Household Cavalry farrier has also been warned of his extra responsibilities." He hesitated and then continued, "On a different matter, I made contact with the gentlemen at Great Western and they are dispatching the rail carriages to Windsor today, in order that any modifications required can be made. I took the liberty of having the requirement of a telegraph installed on both trains …Sir."

"Well done I might as well go back to bed!" I said.

Sergeant O'Keefe laughed.

Just about this time Peter arrived and after being supplied with tea, sat at his desk and brought me up to date on his activities.

He had pulled some strings and had an interview with the Permanent Under Secretary at the Foreign Office. After a similar reception to mine at Horse Guards, Peter had managed to get the Secretary on our side and after viewing the Warrant he could not have been more helpful.

Peter had been taken by a Civil Servant to the bowels of the Foreign Office and shown into an unmarked area of offices, which comprised the cipher department. (A department whose very existence was firmly denied).

The head of the cipher department proceeded to look at the documents Peter had taken with him and quickly assessed one set as to have not been written in code. They were simply written in Punjabi. He passed these documents across to one of his linguists who settled down to translate them.

The second set of documents were, he determined, written in Gaelic and then encrypted. These he stated would take more time to translate. The head cipher clerk called his Irish expert over, a surprisingly young looking man with strikingly red hair and an easy grin. He immediately sat down and studied the documents. By this time, it was about one in the afternoon. Peter stated he must depart for yet another vital meeting, but impressed upon the head of section the urgency of the matter. As Peter was leaving there was a laugh from the Irish expert.

"Got it." He called out. "It is a simple letter replacement code based on a numeric code. Guess the key! '1798'"

They all laughed. (It was the date of the Irish rebellion)

"I should be able to decode these by about 4 this afternoon." The cipher clerk stated. Peter said he would send a courier for them at 4 o'clock.

The time was now 3 so we did not have much time to wait. We dispatched Sergeant O'Keefe to the Foreign Office and Peter and I reviewed what we had achieved if anything to date.

As far as we could see, we had achieved nothing!

At about 4:30 Sergeant O'Keefe arrived with a small package from the Foreign Office.

The only thing of note, as far as they could determine, was from the Gaelic papers and consisted of a letter.

This key letter contained the following information:

John

Had major meeting with Sikhs. They are with us and can provide their portion of funding. They like us, have a man on the inside.

Have explosives and weapons organized and have full itinerary of The British Monarch.

Will sail on SS Augusta Victoria of Hamburg line to Europe. Current sailing time 6 days.

Will make contact once established, via usual channels.

"Oh my God!" I said. "There really is a plot and it has been set in motion! According to the sailing list that ship left a month ago so he has been in Europe for the last three weeks planning whatever he has in mind."

At this moment, Sergeant Borne came in.

"Evening Superintendent, Colonel, I've just got back from the Docklands sir. I have had some of our men watching the area all day. A group was seen entering the warehouse this afternoon; they stayed a couple of hours, then there was a lot of activity, and dozens of boxes were carried out. They finally all left about an hour ago." Sergeant Borne stated

"Good." I said, "We can see how our box worked. If you can arrange for a carriage again we will go around about 2am."

"Very well Sir, leave it to me." Sergeant Borne said.

"Luckily I have brought my tools." I said, tapping my bag.

Later that evening Sergeant Borne and I made the journey to Docklands. We again pulled the coach into the shadows and Sergeant Borne went to confer with his men, to check all was quiet. He came back a few minutes later to say all was well, although a light had been seen in the building at about 9pm, but no one had been seen coming out. Strange, I thought.

I again equipped myself with my waistcoat and dark lamp and moved to the drainpipe. Once again, I checked that it was secure and quickly ascended to the third floor. I checked the window, to make certain it had not been interfered with. Once, I was certain it was safe, I slid it open. I noticed the flour was all scuffed up below the window, as if someone had been standing looking out. I shut the window and sat on the sill for a few moments, gathering my wits and allowing my eyes to grow accustomed to the dark. There was something strange At first I could not place it, then my days on the North West Frontier came back to me and I recognized the smell. It was the smell of spices, in particular curry spices, the smell that lingers on the clothing and breath of someone who eats the particular dishes of the orient. Someone from the Indian continent was in the shadows waiting for me.

I slipped the small cosh that I carried into my sleeve, and then stepped into the room; there was no need to worry about the flour, since my mysterious friend had already scuffed up the flour. The room was a vast storeroom, with large iron columns supporting the ceiling spaced down the centre. I had to pass two of these to reach the stairs.

I moved towards the stairs as if my only concerns were booby traps. I held my trusty trip wire feeler in front of me and slowly advanced across the room. As I passed the second column, I saw some movement out of the corner of my eye. I quickly ducked and swung towards my unknown assailant. He was a turbaned giant of a man who was thrusting a knife in a very expert way towards my back. It was at this stage the lessons I had learnt during my time in China came to the fore. I was able to use his momentum against him, allowing him to flow past me. I then quickly turned him by his wrist, I did this so sharply that with an additional twist, I broke his wrist so ensuring he dropped his knife. Not a sound came from between his lips, even though the breaking of his wrist must have hurt like hell. He came at me again and this time he was out to crush me in a bear like grip. I drove my flat palm under his chin, forcing his head back, my fingers reaching for his eyes. This slowed him down and his good arm went to grab my offending hand and arm. However, I stepped to his injured side and I quickly used my "equalizer" the soft leather cosh filled with lead shot that I had now slipped from my sleeve into my other hand. I dealt him a blow just behind his right ear and I felt his scull crack. Dam, I thought, too hard!

He sank to his knees, stone dead. That created a problem! I will work that out later I thought. However, out of curiosity, I had a look in his mouth and as I suspected his tongue had been cut out. No wonder he had not cried out! I picked up his knife and neatly put it back in his waist sash.

I picked up my trip wire feeler from where I had dropped it and continued towards the stairs I noted none of yesterday's trip wires were in place. I assumed this was so my silent friend would not shoot himself. I even noted the hinged stair had been marked with chalk. This gave me an idea. Despite the lack of traps I did not lower my guard and continued to check for traps.

I got to the office and again checked the door. This time there was no hair or card in the door jam, but on using my mirror I found a penny coin had been left in the office on the inside of the door. I carefully observed its position. I again opened the door and checked around. I detected a trip wire across the floor. It was connected to a concealed gun which was positioned to protect the approach to the safe. I had no intention of going anywhere near that side of the office. I avoided the wire and moved to the grill. I could see that it had not been touched. The screw heads were exactly in the position I had left them and the wax in the grove had not been touched. I removed my box and replaced the grill. I exited the office and checked to see how the penny had been fixed to the door. A small bit of tallow had held it in place. I meticulously reattached it and closed the door.

I went downstairs and checked the door that we had used the day before It was set up in exactly the same way. This was a relief since I now knew there would be no problem in me cautiously opening it and handing Sergeant Borne the box. I explained there had been a problem and I needed his help. He was to deposit the box in the coach and have one of his men guard it, and then come back. This he did with the minimum of questions. We cautiously then went up the stairs and moved the dead Sikh: for that is what he was, to the stairs. I carefully positioned his body just above the booby-trapped stair tread and held him in position with a broom. As soon as Sergeant Borne was out of the way, I removed the broom and ran down the remaining stairs. The Sikh's body slid on to the stair tread. Triggering the catch, this collapsed that flight of stairs and sent his body down three floors to the solid concrete basement floor below. It hit the concrete with a sickening "thwack," I hoped that anyone finding him would think he had accidentally stood on the tread and plummeted to his death.

We exited and made our way back to the safety of the Palace and our office. Sergeant O'Keefe, had some how gained access to another room in the cellars and furnished it with beds, carpets etc. It was better furnished than my room in the club. I noted the rugs alone were worth more than my annual salary. I decided I had better rein in Sergeant O'Keefe before some of the Crown Jewels started appearing in our rooms as door stops! Peter was fast asleep in a bed that had sheets with the Royal Crest embroidered upon them. Next to the bed was a side table with a crystal glass again with the Royal Monogram. I quickly woke him, as Sergeant O'Keefe went to rustle up some tea and get the carriage taken care of. I was rather worried what china the tea would appear in!

On returning to the office, I methodically checked the box and determined that none of the seals I had put in place had been tampered with, this confirmed that the box had not been discovered. I opened it and found the cylinder had been activated and by the scratches on the wax drum, it had recorded something.

I rewound it and moved the lever to the play position. At this stage, Peter and Sergeant O'Keefe reappeared. Sergeant O'Keefe with four mugs: I was relieved to note without a Royal Monogram, of tea. The Royal Kitchens obviously never closed!

"Right Gentlemen let's hear what we can hear. I don't know how the quality is going to be, but hopefully we should get something useful." I said, sounding more confident than I felt

I pulled the start lever and the disk started turning. It was like listening to someone talking inside a tent with a hailstorm going on outside and the hailstones drumming on the canvas. We sat in silence for the first play through. Each of us concentrating on trying to pick up the words.

"Well, there is definitely something there and they certainly mentioned the Queen, the Palace, our man and France." Peter stated.

"Yes I got that as well. Let's start again and try playing small parts with each of us writing down what we think was said." I suggested

It was about 10am when we finally all sat back in our chairs and felt we had the gist of what had been recorded.

As far as we could tell, there were four men in the room talking. The one leading the conversation, we thought, had a Dublin accent, and there was another individual present, with an Indian accent.

It appeared from the conversation, that they had discovered that the Palace had found out about the plot and that a team (us) was trying to stop them. They appeared to know I was involved, which caused the Indian to say some very unpleasant things in Punjabi.

Their contact in the Palace it appeared had not been able to find out what we were planning, or even what we had discovered to date (this was gratifying). However, I decided, that henceforth, the office would never be unlocked or unattended.

The plotters suspected that someone had tried to enter the warehouse the night before, but did not think we had got into the office. However, as a precaution, they were going to move their base and were going to booby trap the safe, so that if it were opened it would explode! They were also going to leave a welcoming committee in case (my silent friend!) someone visited.

Finally, they appeared to agree that the plot was still viable and that from now on they would not meet, but only communicate in the usual way, that is "The Times" personal column

There was no more that we could glean; we could not work out if the attack was to be in Britain or the Continent. The most worrying things were that they were confident despite the fact that they knew we were on to them and that they had a spy in the Palace.

We only had a few more days before the Queen left Windsor Castle for the continent; we therefore decided we must split our forces. Sergeant O'Keefe and I would leave for Windsor and put in hand the protective measures for her Majesty.

Peter and Sergeant Borne would work on trying to detect what was going on; in particular, they would try to find out whom the contact in the Palace was. They would also attempt to discover the nature of the messages placed in "The Times" that were used to pass their clandestine messages to one another.

Chapter 5

Windsor

Sergeant O'Keefe and I left for Windsor that very day, taking the first express train of the day to Windsor Station. Lieutenant Scott- Hamilton, the troop Commander of the Grenadier Guards Troop, greeted us there. He snapped off a salute that only a Guards Officer can master, but the resentment of being put under the command of a Royal Engineer even though he was a Colonel was evident. I kept my own counsel. When we arrived at Windsor Castle I was shown my quarters. Lieutenant Scott-Hamilton made to melt away at this stage, muttering something about a dinner engagement. I told him to cancel it and get the Officer of the Lancers; they were both to meet me in half an hour in whatever office they had arranged for me. By the look of the Lieutenant's face, no office had been arranged.

"Leave the office to me!" Sergeant O'Keefe stated.

"Very well! Half an hour Scott-Hamilton --- you are dismissed Sir!" I barked before he could object.

About 20 minutes later Sergeant O'Keefe came back in.

"Your office awaits Sir, and I've sent an orderly for that idiot; with all due respect, and the Sikh Officer Sir..." Sergeant O'Keefe stated

"Thank you Sergeant O'Keefe, I need to use that Warrant that we have been given. The only way you are going to get respect in the Guards is by rank Mr. O'Keefe!"

"Pardon Sir?" He said in a very rare moment of amazement.

"I said Mr. O'Keefe Warrant Officer Class One!" I said with a quick smile.

"Can you get the rank on your Uniform in the next 10 minutes Mr. O'Keefe?" I asked.

"Is the Pope Catholic Sir?" He declared.

"Where is the office?" I asked.

Mr. O'Keefe told me and I made my way down by myself allowing Mr. O'Keefe a little more time to get his uniform amended.

I found I had been given a neat but incredibly small office. It did remind me of a hastily converted stable! However, it was an office and we could not be overheard.

There was a knock on the door and Mr. O'Keefe sporting his new rank put his head around the door.

"Lieutenant Scott-Hamilton and Captain Nawaab Kapoor Singh Sir." Mr. O'Keefe announced

"Show them in please Mr. O'Keefe and please stay outside to ensure we are not overheard." I replied.

"Certainly Sir." He said.

A resentful Lieutenant and a very smart Sikh Captain marched into the office.

I looked at the Lieutenant and acknowledged his salute, then turned to the Captain.

"What was your name again Captain?" I asked.

"Captain Nawaab Kapoor Singh Colonel Saab." He replied.

He somehow looked familiar and I asked, "Are you related to Captain Kapoor Singh of the Ist Sikh Infantry?"

"Yes Colonel he was my father." He said finding it hard not to hide his pleasure as being recognized.

"A great man Captain, I had the honour of serving with him in the second Afghan War" I stated.

"I know Colonel, you saved his life." The Captain replied.

"He exaggerated we helped each other!" I said with a smile.

"Colonel, he spoke often of you as the most inspiring officer he had ever served under, the bravest and a true friend." The Captain said.

"How is he now?" I asked.

"He was killed a year a go by rebels disloyal to the Queen and Empress." He said in a sad but proud voice.

"I'm so sorry, I did not know." I said, rather embarrassed at having raised such a sad subject.

"That is alright Sir; it is an honour to serve with you as my Father did." The Captain said, drawing himself up to his full impressive 6 feet 1 inch height.

I paused for a moment, and looked at the two officers both as different as could be but both proud and owing total loyalty to Her Majesty.

"Gentlemen please read these." I stated.

I handed the Warrant and the Home Secretary's letters across the table to them.

They each read one in silence, and then handed it across to the other, taking the other document in exchange. When they had both read each document, they handed the documents reverently back to me.

"Gentlemen, putting it simply we and by that I mean Superintendent Smither, Sergeant Borne, Mr. O'Keefe, yourselves, your men and myself have been charged with one task. In the next month, her Majesty is going to be attacked by a group of Irish and Sikh extremists with the intent of either killing her or kidnapping her or even both. This is not to happen! In order to prevent this we are to ensure our men are as highly trained as we can possibly make them. This means no more dinner parties Lieutenant. We have until Tuesday morning, when the Queen departs on her journey to get our men fully prepared. We have much to do and we will start at 0800hrs tomorrow."

"Any questions" I asked.

Both officers stood in stunned silence.

First, to speak was the Captain.

"Sir I am a Sikh as are my men and yet you still trust me!" He said.

"Of course! You are your father's son! Oh but if you should betray me I would hunt you down to the ends of the earth and kill you!" I replied

He grinned. "My father was correct you are a man to follow."

"Lieutenant any questions?" I asked turning towards Scott-Hamilton

"I'm sorry Colonel I never realized..." He began.

"Enough." I said. "Gentlemen tomorrow at 8am dressed for the field goodnight."

At the appointed hour, the next morning the platoon of Grenadiers and The troop of Lancers were on parade ready for inspection. I inspected and spoke to every one looking them square in the eye and trying to gauge the individual's metal.

After my inspection, I had a conference with the two Officers and their Senior NCOs'

I explained to them once again the urgency of the task we had been given and the fact we had a very short time to get ready. I also explained that the task was made more complex; her Majesty had stated she did not want any more security and that she was not to be inconvenienced. We had informed her therefore, via Sir Harry, that the role of soldiers who were accompanying her was to put on Military displays. In the case of the Lancers their prowess with their lances. They needed to ensure they had a good tent pegging display arranged. Captain Singh nodded in understanding.

The Guards were to put on a marching display. Scott-Hamilton looked to his Colour Sergeant who gave a confident nod.

I continued "So much for the cover story. Now the real tasks I want from both of you is to detail your five best men to me. They must be crack shots, be able to climb a rope unaided and oh yes be able to swim fully clothed. I have arranged for all your men Lieutenant Scott-Hamilton to be issued with grey suits which they are to wear at night when on guard. I have arranged for Gieves and Hawkes to tailor one for you and the Captain."

"I have also arranged that we will all be issued with the new protype Webley six shot black powder cartridge revolvers They have enough stopping power to stop a water buffalo so should stop a charging Irishman or Sikh. The armourer will be around this afternoon to fit everyone to his revolver." I drew my revolver from its holster so they could see what I meant. The revolver had been modified in that the trigger guard had been removed to allow quick and easy access and the spur on the hammer had been removed to prevent the chance of it catching in clothing when being removed from a pocket or holster. The grip was also unique. The armourer had taken a molding of my grip and then carved my grip into the handle of the gun. Even in the darkest of nights, I would always grip the pistol in the same way ensuring complete consistency of shooting.

Both Officers looked puzzled but acquiesced.

"You have today to conduct your own training tomorrow we will put it all together!"

"Any questions? Good." With that, I left the room and allowed them to scratch their collective heads.

For the next three days, we all worked 18 hours a day. Jumping off trains and jumping on trains. Running into carriages and fighting from compartment to compartment. The soldiers loved it having an excuse to have a raw house and generally hit each other. When Her Majesty was away, we used part of the Castle as if it was the hotel the Queen was going to stay in. Again, and again, we practiced storming into the building rescuing the Queen, played by one of her maids, running out, putting her in a carriage, and galloping off. By the giggles from the maid, she enjoyed every moment. All the soldiers had been issued with their revolvers and hours were spent on the ranges. They worked in pairs to become efficient marksmen at close quarters both day and night. Not only were they expected to be able to hit a running man at 10 yards in the dark they also had to be able to reload the weapon in the time it took their partner to fire three aimed shots.

The Guardsmen had been issued with their grey suits, rubber soled boots, and after I trained Lieutenant Scott-Hamilton in the art of stealthy sentry duty, the art of merging with shadows and generally not standing out so a prospective assailant knew where the guard was. He quickly grasped the idea and instructed his men accordingly. Once again, interesting exercises took place with half the Guardsmen trying to infiltrate their now invisible compatriots. A rough house did develop on several occasions and it cost us a few more grey suits but the results were worth it.

Finally, I assembled the soldiers who had been nominated as the rope climbers on the roof and taught them the Tibetan way of using a rope as a friction break to take their weight as they slid down the rope and through open windows.

Each night we held a progress meeting, then fell into a deep, and well earned sleep.

I kept in touch with Peter via telegraph and made use of the Royal Courier who brought mail from the Palace every day. Peter sent a detailed report of his progress daily.

It was from these reports that I learnt of Peter's successes and failures.

After Warrant Officer Class 1 O'Keefe, as he now was and I had left for Windsor, Peter and Sergeant Borne had decided that there best course of action was to try to put pressure on the man they had in gaol. Unfortunately, they found out almost immediately that he had been discovered hanging in his cell; the Fenians had extracted their revenge. The next set back was the warehouse, the scene of our only success to date. It had mysteriously caught fire and the interior had been destroyed. An unidentified and unrecognizable body was found in the cellars; it was burnt to a crisp. The plotters were obviously closing their stable doors.

Peter had decided he needed help and had gone back to the cipher department of the Foreign Office. He had explained that he knew the plotters were using the personal columns of "The Times", as a means of communication but did not have the resources to find out how. Could they help? They immediately put both their Irish and Punjabi experts onto the project and they started scanning the personal columns for the past month to see if they could spot any messages and work out what they meant.

With that in hand, Peter and Sergeant Borne turned their attention to the spy within the Palace. After the obvious strageum of checking if anyone had been employed in the last two months with an Irish or Indian background had turned up blank, Peter decided he would try to force the individual into the open. They used the Constable who was the telegraph operator to drop some indiscrete remarks in the royal kitchens about how the office was frequently left un-attended because they were so understaffed, particularly at night. He also let slip how when he went off duty he left the telegraphs we had sent and their replies on our desks.

Peter then used my box to good effect; he hid it in the office having primed it, in the hope that we could identify who if anyone came in. He ensured the first night there was nothing of any intelligence value about but did leave some false telegraphs all predicting some vital information would come in the next 24 hours.

The next morning, Peter checked the box and was delighted to find his ploy had worked and someone had been into the room. In fact, it was even better since there were two people. He managed to identify the individuals as being the secretary to Sir Harry and the other, the trusted Sikh secretary to her Majesty who was visiting from Windsor Castle.

Chapter 6

Jeremiah was angry, no he wasn't he was furious, a whole year's planning, coordinating and plotting had been put at risk just because some idiot woman had gossiped to another and this had been overheard and ended up in a letter addressed to the very person who was to be the victim! Worse still rather than disregarding it as the meaningless prattle of a silly woman the comment had been acted upon and a team from The Special Branch were at this very moment trying to find if there was any truth in this chitchat.

If this was not enough, the people who had been tasked with the investigation appeared to know their business and had discovered the warehouse in the docks. That was thanks to that idiot Murray. Well, at least he had been taken care of and was swinging in his cell as a lesson to any other informants.

As far as he could tell, these bloody Special Branch people had not discovered anything from the warehouse. Yes, they would know now that John owned it, and the fact that it was so well protected must have raised their suspicions. They clearly had not managed to get into the safe so that is why they tried the next day and met Ramgarhia. He was still amazed that, who ever it was, who had broken in, had managed to survive an attack by Ramgarhia and even kill him; it showed they must be good.

So, should he continue? He was well set up in a safe location and ready to act. Clearly, he felt the authorities did not have any idea of his plans. Nor, did they have any idea that he had spies in the Palace feeding him with up to date information. Nor, did they know how he communicated with the others. Yes, they probably were putting in some extra protection and his source had indicated that there was a lot of extra activity at Windsor Castle, and some additional train carriages had arrived. It would appear they were planning to add to the Royal Train. That would not affect the plan. Therefore, overall whilst there had been a set back it was not going to affect the success of the mission. The kidnapping of the Queen, ransoming her for the diamond and then killing her could still go ahead. The Sikhs would not share the value of the diamond and so he would get nothing without the killing of the Queen. This, he believed would obviously end her reign and bring to the throne her weak son who would be easy to intimidate. Yes, overall, the plans were still good and he had enough back up contingency plans if the first attempt failed. Overall, he was confident of success. However just to be certain Jeremiah felt it might be worth teaching these Special Branch people a lesson. Rather than a lesson, just wiping them out of the equation once and for all.

Whether Jeremiah would have been so confident if he knew that we had discovered more than he thought is open to debate.

Chapter 7

Peter had sent a telegram to me, in which he asked to meet as soon as possible. I had replied by Royal Courier, who happened to be going that very hour, that I could be there at 8pm and would bring Mr. O'Keefe.

I checked that the training was in hand and that Lieutenant Scott-Hamilton had not tried to arrange a dinner party! Just to be on the safe side I had his batman hide Mr. Scott-Hamilton's formal dinner clothes.

I grabbed my bag of tools and this time also my new revolver and accompanied by Mr. O'Keefe set off by express train for the Palace. Peter had arranged for a carriage to meet us and soon we were galloping along to yet another side door.

We went to our office and Mr. O'Keefe went in search of a cold platter of food and some tea for us. On his successful return, we all tucked into some cold beef, mustard and bread whilst Peter brought us up to date. He was now certain who the spies were in the Royal Household. Further, the Foreign Office were confident they had discovered how messages were being sent and the code that was used. They also felt they could duplicate the messages to send their own without the deception being noticed. If fact they had spotted a new message in today's Times but had not at this stage had a chance to turn their attention to it.

Peter explained how he had had the idea either of trying to get the informants to work for us knowingly or by feeding them false information. Cracking the codes had meant we did not really need their cooperation any more. However, the question was did we want them on the loose?

We were generally mulling this over when I looked absently at the wall clock that Mr.

O'Keefe had acquired all those days ago. It seemed a lifetime ago now. I looked at the clock and something began to niggle in the back of my mind. The clock had stopped. This I assumed was because Mr. O'Keefe was not here to check on such details. Still my mind kept nagging at something. Why was I concerned that the clock had stopped. Peter noticed that I was wearing a puzzled frown.

"What's the matter? Don't you like the idea of keeping them free?" He asked.

"No it's not that, there is something about this room that is wrong." I said in a distracted manner.

Peter said. "Sorry to hurry you but time is tight!"

"That's it!" I exclaimed. "Quiet, everyone listen! Can you hear ticking?"

"Of course it's the clock..."Peter began to say, and then realized like me the clock had stopped but there was still something in the room ticking!

We all jumped to our feet and started frantically searching the room. For such a small room there were an amazing number of built in cupboards and obviously also the furniture we had put in. Finally, we tracked the ticking to a floor level cupboard that had been designed to hold decanters. Behind a row of empty decanters was a long brown cardboard box. I asked Peter to pass my bag and then for them to get out of the room. Mr. O'Keefe refused saying he would pass the tools to me and anyway there was only ¾ of him left anyway.

I smiled "Thanks, Mr. O'Keefe. Remind me to speak to the pay master and ensure you are put on ¾ pay."

"Me and my mouth." He ruefully replied with a smile.

Having got on my stomach I crawled in to the cupboard and used a small mirror that Mr. O'Keefe passed me to look into the box and all around it. It did not seem to be booby trapped so I managed to pull it into the open. Inside the box there was a clock wired to some electric battery cells and wired to an electric detonator, which was pushed into a large block of gun cotton.

I checked the clock and saw that the timer was set to go off at 9pm. It was now 8.55pm I quickly reached in and pulled the detonator out of the gun cotton and just to make certain I started to undo the terminals on the battery. It was whilst I was doing this I heard a crack and the detonator went off sending a shower of sparks and copper fragments into my arm. The clock was fast!

I grinned at Mr. O'Keefe and said,

"Woops!"

"One day sir, just one day you will really hurt me!" It was the closest he would ever come to saying well done! "I'll just go and get some hot water and some dressings for your arm Sir." He uttered leaving the room.

"Right Peter, I think it would seem we are really getting close! The fact they actually want to blow us up would indicate that we are having a negative effect upon them!" I said resuming my seat.

"It strikes me you have a negative effect on most people!" Peter said with a grin.

"Anyway I think that gave us our next step. We can write their code now…yes?" I asked

"Yes!" Peter replied.

"Right, we bring the spies in and we make certain no one but no one knows or can get near them! Probably the Tower is the answer in this particular case." I said and then continued. "We will then send a message, via The Times, that their attack was a success and the team leaders have been killed, but that we the spies were spotted and so are going into hiding." I said.

"Sounds good to me." Said Peter.

"Oh yes I have a present for you and Sergeant borne." I said and handed a Webley Revolver to both Peter and Sergeant Borne." You know how to use these don't you?"

"Probably not as well as you but certainly well enough to make a very large hole in a man's abdomen at 10 paces." Peter said expertly stripping the gun then reassembling it making certain all chambers were fully charged.

After that, we moved with surprising speed. Whilst I got my arm, cleaned and dressed Peter organized a special branch carriage and team of armed constables to surround and take Sir Harry's secretary. He put up very little fight but there again waking up with the barrel of a revolver behind your ear and another up your nostril is generally guaranteed to get compliance!

Her Majesty's Sikh secretary was a little more slippery. He was awake when we pounced on his quarters in Windsor castle and he managed to evade the efforts of the constables. He ran out of his quarters towards the Queens private chambers, screaming that he would kill the false Empress of India." His way was blocked by Captain Singh

"You bring disgrace on our people!" Captain Singh shouted at the secretary.

"You lap dog! You are the one who brings disgrace!" With that, the secretary drew a sabre and charged the captain.

The clash was short but truly bloody. The secretary's weapon of choice was a pen not a sabre! The Captain parried the clumsy attacks then went in for the kill cutting and cutting again shouting as he did:

"That is for my father, this is for my People, this is for my Men and this final cut is for my Empress!"

I thought it was rather melodramatic but never the less a fine display of swordsmanship!

Chapter 8

On Tuesday 14th, the Queen was driven by covered carriage, with a pair of greys pulling, to the railway station. Captain Singh and I had exchanged positions with the true equerries, Sir Carstairs McNeill and Captain Edwards and were riding directly behind the carriage, scanning the cheering crowd for any sign of trouble. We had managed to get the Queen to agree not to allow the public within the confines of the Railway station. I had sent Lt Scott-Hamilton ahead and his role was to search the Royal Train inside and out whilst the Lancers secured the outer parameter.

The Royal party consisted of; Her Majesty, Princess Beatrice, Major General Sir Henry Ponsonby, Lord Bridport, Equerry, Lady Churchill, Lady in Waiting, The Hon. Victoria Baille, Lady in Waiting and the Queen's Doctor, Doctor Reid. Also traveling on the train were John Brown and the usual selection of servant's valets and maids as well as kitchen staff for the train's kitchen. On top of this, I had managed to include Lt Scott-Hamilton and five of his best men.

The Royal train set off five minutes late at 10:20am, whilst just one hundred yards in front was our train. We had men on the front and rear of the train scanning the line for obstacles and the surrounding countryside for suspicious activity. The men at the rear of the train kept a careful watch of the Royal Train to ensure it did not slow down or speed up. They were in contact with our locomotive by a ship like telegraph. This indicated go, forward, back, speed up, slow down, and stop.

Inside our train was an atmosphere of suppressed excitement. The Lancers stood next to their fully saddled mounts ready at a moment's notice to leap from the train. The Guardsmen were in a similar state of readiness.

As it turned out, the journey was uneventful and we arrived in Portsmouth at 12:30pm. Captain Singh immediately busied himself with getting his men and mounts on the ship we had arranged for him to get across the Channel in. The plan was for him to sail ahead of us and secure the Queen's continental train and the pier where the Queen was due to disembark.

At the same time I contacted Peter by telegram to see if there had been any further developments. We had decided that the best course of action was for him and Sergeant Borne to continue their investigations, whilst I took charge of the Her Majesty's protection.

Peter had already sent a telegram saying he had heard from the Sussex Police and that the Hall where the Sikhs had been living had been vacated for the last two weeks. The whole household appeared to have moved out in great haste for an undisclosed destination. He had also heard from India. Brigadier Long reported a group of Sikh extremists had been spirited out of the Punjab and were, it was believed, on their way to England. It was thought the Russians had been involved in helping them on route to Europe, via Afghanistan.

Peter further reported that he was making some progress on tracing the people behind the plot. Having lost our original lead, he had gone back to what we knew, that was that they were using "The Times" as a means of communication. He had discovered that the messages were actually left at the Times Office, either by mail or in person. He assumed this was dependent upon the urgency of the message.

He felt our false messages would engender a rapid response, so he had had "The Times" offices under close surveillance. This had paid off in that his men had spotted a well know Fenian supporter enter the offices and leave a message for publication in the personal column. They had followed him to his lodging and were now keeping him under very close observation. Peters next move was to send another message, this time from "our man in the tower" asking for urgent help. He hoped this would allow us to find out how the messages got to the messenger and lead us to someone more senior in their organization.

Having communicated to Peter, congratulating him on his work and reassuring him that everything seemed to be going to plan, I returned to the harbour and was pleased to find Mr. Parsons himself at the port. He met me with a smile and a hearty handshake.

His boat was in a covered slip way and he led the way alongside it. It had magnificent lines and since I had last seen it, had grown a forward deck gun and a powerful search light. Mr. Parsons then introduced the crew, consisting of some very handy looking sailors who looked like they could sail around the "Horn" in their sleep. The skipper was even more impressive, it was Mr. Parsons himself.

I smiled, I knew better than protest. I told him we were due to set sail as soon as The Royal Yacht Victoria and Albert had taken on board its precious cargo. I left him organizing the getting up of steam and went to get my crew and speak to Lt Scott-Hamilton. He had the task of mounting guard on the ship, for the crossing and managing the watch through the night. I would stay on board the turbine boat until the Queen disembarked the next morning.

The Yacht weighed anchor and with much saluting, rising, and lowering of flags ensigns and standards the flotilla set sail across the channel to Cherbourg. The channel was as smooth as glass and the visibility outstanding. Again, like the train journey the journey went without incident. It must have been frustrating for Mr. Parsons, who like me really wanted to open the throttles of his vessel, but he had to be contented to potter along at a sedate 9 knots.

We arrived in Cherbourg and the yacht anchored a couple of hundred yards out into the harbour. The Queen and the Royal party stayed on board and had a banquet. I briefly went ashore to speak to Captain Singh and he confirmed the train was secured and that there was considerable activity on the pier for the welcome tomorrow of the Queen. He had heard a strange report from one of his men, who had spoken to some town official. This official had made the odd comment that the Sikh troop was the second group of men with turbans in the town in the last week!

On hearing this I moved back to the boat and told them I was going to base myself on the yacht tonight and that Mr. O'Keefe was to take charge of the soldiers on the turbine vessel. I then hailed a tender from the yacht and went aboard. I found Lieutenant Scott-Hamilton in full mess dress.

"What are you doing Scott-Hamilton?" I asked in an incredulous voice.

"Oh, I've been requested too join the Royal party for Dinner, Sir." He replied beaming with pleasure.

"Who, is in charge of the men?" I asked.

"Oh my Colour Sergeant, he is very good at guard mounting" Scott-Hamilton stated dismissively.

"Just get out of my sight!" I said, having smelt the alcohol on his breath; I decided he would be a liability rather than an asset.

I went in search of the Colour Sergeant and hoped he was more professional than his officer had turned out to be. As I stormed down the deck, I spotted some moment behind a lifeboat. I found the Colour Sergeant inspecting his men in preparation of them going on guard for the evening. They were in full uniform including their red tunics. I stood and gaped. Actually, I stood and fumed.

"Colour, could I have a word please?" I said, coming up behind him.

He turned and I was pleased to see a flood of relief come over his face, as opposed to contempt or any other emotion.

"Colonel, thank goodness you are here." The colour sergeant blurted out, before he remembered his loyalties. "Sorry Sir, could I have a quick word in private."

"Certainly Colour, just dismiss the men and tell them to get correctly dressed for night duty please!" I replied.

"Yes Sir! You heard the officer back here in 15 minutes dressed for night duty - grey suits and revolvers. Officer on Parade fall out." He barked. The men turned sharply to the right saluted and quickly dispersed.

"Right Colour, you have five minutes to tell me what has been going on."

He drew a deep breath steeling himself to be disloyal to his officer, I interrupted. "Look Colour, there is more than regimental pride at stake, we are here to prevent an attack on the Queen and I have a strong feeling an attack is about to happen."

This decided him. "Sir, as soon as you left Mr. Scott-Hamilton alone, he countered all your orders. He said it was all poppy cock and you did not know what you were talking about. He said we were Guardsmen and would act as Guardsmen and dress accordingly, Sir."

"And what do you think Colour?" I asked.

"Sir, I was in Afghanistan and China and I have heard of you. I know you know soldiering. I tried to tell him, Sir, but he told me to mind my place." The Colour Sergeant replied.

"Thank you for your frankness Colour". Right lets sort this mess out. I have a feeling we are going to have visitors tonight. Post your men and make certain they are in different potions than they were in since we anchored. I am certain we have been observed. I would imagine the Sikhs and their friends will attack in two groups to try to split us. When it happens, you take two of your best men and guard the Royal Chambers or wherever Her Majesty is. Warn the men these people will not hesitate; they are all highly experienced and motivated killers. Once they attack we will set off a firework display from the top of the ship, this will cover our gun fire and act as a signal to our other forces that we are under attack."

"Right Sir and thank you." The Colour Sergeant replied.

"What for?" I asked.

"Not replacing me with Mr. O'Keefe sir." He replied.

"You might come to regret that I didn't." I replied.

The men were now assembling. I gave them a pep talk and checked their weapons were all loaded. I then handed them over to the Colour Sergeant to "post" them. I asked him to detail one man to be positioned on the upper deck. His job on hearing the first shot fired was to set off the rocket firework display that I had set up. I also made it clear that on the first sign or sound of trouble all off duty men were to rally on me. I would be blowing a whistle.

I took up position on the rear quarterdeck by a large vent and stood in its shadow waiting for what I felt the inevitable attack. Inside the main stateroom I could hear lively conversation and music from the Marine Band.

Having stood in the darkness for some time my eyes and ears were accustomed to the night. I heard a muffled noise from the stern of the ship and realized it was stealthy rowing of a boat was approaching. There was a thud and a rag-covered grappling hook landed on the deck. Someone then started to pull the rope back, dragging the grappling hook to the rail where it sank its tangs into the highly polished wooden planking of the deck.

I drew my razor sharp kukri and was about to approach the rail and cut the rope, when the doors of the stateroom were flung open banging against the adjoining bulkheads. Lieutenant Scott-Hamilton stood in the opening blowing a stream of smoke from his cigar; he staggered unsteadily across the deck, holding a large Brandy Balloon and the cigar. He was approaching the rail oblivious of the grapnel, or me. He was making a frightful din calling out for the guard to fall in for inspection.

"Colour, Colour where the hell are you man." He was shouting.

He had distracted me for a couple of moments, but this was all it took for the first climber to reach the deck. A head popped over the rail. The climber made a quick "sweep of the deck" saw Lt Scott-Hamilton and ducked down. Scott-Hamilton must have seen some movement, because he froze in mid stride. The head reappeared and an arm came arching over it throwing a knife expertly into Scott-Hamilton's neck. It effectively stopped him in his tracks and prevented any sound escaping from his lips. He dropped both the cigar and brandy balloon. Making futile clawing motions with his hands at the knife he fell to his knees. The Sikh assailant, for that was what he was, pulled himself onto the deck in an instant running silently across to the body of Scott-Hamilton and pulling his knife out of the stricken lieutenant's neck. The assassin then carefully looked around him. This was as far as he got, because I had left the cover of my vent and was now directly behind him. I quickly placed the barrel of my revolver behind his right ear and pulled the trigger. I did not pause to see the results, I was already sprinting to the rail leaning over and discharging my revolver into the face of the next Sikh on the rope. At the same time, I used my kukri to sever the rope. There was a satisfactory splash as the individuals on the rope disappeared into the darkness below.

I now pulled out my whistle and blew it for all I was worth. I was quickly joined by the nearest sentry, who careful not to silhouette himself, took charge of the stern of the ship. The off duty men came running out of the nearest doorway and

I quickly detained two to stay with the sentry. We then formed an extended line and with me leading we advanced up the ships deck to the bow. The soldier detailed to set off the rockets had done his job magnificently and they were soaring into the sky. I did not have time to say "oow" and "arr" but they were impressive!

I now heard firing from the bow. I had to assume that the Colour Sergeant had that area under control. I was pleased to see someone was thinking because the lights in the stateroom where the Queen was enjoying the banquet in her honour has been dowsed. There was still considerable shooting and shouting from the other end of the vessel and we were getting closer. As we approached, we started shouting out "Grenadiers" repeatedly so that our own men would not shoot us. Two or three turbaned figures came running out of the shadows towards us firing some rifles but the space was too confined for them to get an aimed shot and the Grenadiers quickly put them to rest with well-aimed revolver fire.

We met up with the soldiers at the bow of the ship and they explained how as instructed on the first shot being fired, Colour had taken two men and doubled to the stateroom to protect the Queen. It was at this stage that another shot rang out from behind us. I turned and ran towards the shooting calling for a section to follow me. We ran down the stairs that connected to the passageway leading to the Stateroom. Lying in a pool of blood was a Guardsman who feebly pointed ahead gasping the Colour Sergeant was chasing two Sikhs.

We reached a corner and the stateroom doors were ahead. One Sikh had turned and was blazing away at Colour and the other Guardsman. The other Sikh was hammering at the door with the butt of a rifle. As we arrived along side Colour, the doors of the stateroom burst inwards. However, in his efforts the Sikh had broken the stock of his rifle. He threw it down, drew a large throwing knife, and advanced into the room.

We redoubled our efforts and finally managed to subdue the Sikh guard and went charging into the stateroom revolvers at the ready.

The Sikh had spotted Her Majesty and swung his arm back to fling his knife at her. Suddenly a loan slim and very attractive female figure stood up and very calmly fired an Adams revolver at him hitting him squarely in the forehead. He dropped on to the dining table stone dead.

I looked at the lady who had shot the Sikh and as calmly as I could, said

"Nicola, how many times have I told you, body shot, not head shot?"

The Colour Sergeant was by this time at my shoulder, "Colonel, that is no was to address Princess Beatrice." He stated in a shocked voice.

"True, but it is not Princess Beatrice. Allow me to introduce Miss Nicola Ryan, a female colleague from the Special Branch. I had managed to convince her Majesty that we needed one last line of defence!" I said. "By the way, is that all of them?"

"Yes Sir, these two had got aboard before we spotted them. The others are dead and we heard rowing moving away from the ship so can assume they have departed for now." The Colour Sergeant replied.

"Then it is Mr. O'Keefe's problem now." I said.

"Your Majesty, are you all right?" I asked

She seemed to be in a slight state of shock. She kept saying "Oh a trifle a trifle."

"No, you Majesty." I said, "It was not a trifle, they were trying to kill you!

"No Colonel, I mean that Sikh has fallen in my trifle!" she exclaimed.

Before I could think of a fitting reply, the sound of naval gunfire penetrated the oak lined walls of the stateroom and the powerful spotlight of Mr. Parson's ship could be seen sweeping across the water, we rushed to the deck to see what was going on.

Mr. O'Keefe explained later what had happened.

On seeing the fireworks display, Mr. O'Keefe knew that something was terribly wrong. With Mr. Parsons at the helm they had crept forward into the harbour. There seemed to be some kind of fight on the harbour wall, just by where one of the torpedo boats was moored. Almost instantly they saw the boat pulling away. There were sparks and smoke pouring out of its single funnel and it appeared to be trying get up to its maximum speed very quickly. A lone whaler had managed to get along side it and a few figures were seen to clamber on board.

Mr. Parsons smiled and murmur, "If they think they can get away from me in that they are sadly mistaken."

He was about to open the throttles wide, when Mr. O'Keefe realized what was going on.

"Sir, they are not trying to get away, look they are trying to get into a position to torpedo the Royal Yacht." He screamed.

"Oh no they don't," Mr. Parsons Shouted. He yelled to his men to man the gun and train the spotlight on the torpedo boat. He then opened the throttles and the boat shot forward, rapidly accelerating to its 34-knot maximum speed.

The crew who were holding on for grim death managed to keep the spotlight on the torpedo boat. There seemed to be a mixture of Sikhs and Europeans on board. They all appeared to be working with one aim and that was to fire a torpedo at the Royal Yacht. The spotlight was making it hard for them since it was blinding them and Mr Parsons' fast approach between the Sikhs and the Yacht meant they could not get a straight shot. Mr. Parsons' forward gun began to fire and despite the speed of the boat the aim was true and within two shots Mr Parsons' men was scoring hits. The second shell hit the torpedo boat's torpedo tube, there was a blinding flash, and the torpedo boat and its crew disappeared completely. Mr. Parsons reduced speed to look for survivors, but none was found.

So ended the first night of the Queens vacation!

Extracts of correspondence of the day

Extract of letter from Queen Victoria

My Dearest Bertie

Our journey to the South of France has commenced and we enjoyed a most leisurely train journey from Windsor to the coast. The train kept at a very safe speed and I did not in the least feel worried for ourself or our household.

The Yacht Victoria and Albert provided us with a glorious cruise across the channel. The sea was beautifully calm and a charming emerald green. We were surrounded by delightfully little naval ships, which dashed around us like small sheep dogs around a flock keeping us both safe and entertained.

On arriving at Cherbourg we hosted an intimate dinner party but regret to say we were displeased by the conduct of the young Grenadier Officer who appeared to become the worse for drink! If your dear father had been alive, he would have dealt severely with the young man and he would have left suitably chastised. As it happened, we did have a number of uninvited guests at the dinner and he fell foul of their activities. However, I am pleased that my other travel companions are both charming and resourceful. The Colonel of Engineers and a young lady traveling with me both showed considerable resolve and politely ensured that I was not subject to these interlopers unwelcome approaches.

The evening concluded with a most diverting fireworks display and a boat race, which I am pleased to say, was won by Mr. Charles Parsons. Your dear Papa would have been vastly entertained.

Tomorrow we attend an official reception in our honour then we continue our journey by train to the South of France.

I do hope you are behaving yourself, one hears such unpleasant rumours about your conduct that I clearly do not give credence too, but….

Please do not smoke too many of those horrid cheap cigars, if you are not careful someone will name the beastly things after you!

Your every loving

Victoria Regina

Diary entry of Jeremiah O'Donovan Rossa dated 16th March 1882

Have just heard that the attempted kidnapping of Queen Victoria at Cherbourg was an unmitigated disaster. The Sikhs managed to get aboard the Yacht but rather than simply killing the guard, in a way they are master, the sentries killed them. It appears the Sentries were hidden and not dressed in their red tunics. The one Sikh who managed to get away said they were led by a Colonel who seemed to know the ways of tribal fighting and is totally ruthless in his resolve to protect the Queen.

Then, when my men captured a torpedo boat and were going to torpedo the yacht another unidentified boat came out of nowhere and traveling at an impossibly fast speed overtook them and sank them.

I am of the opinion these must be the same Special Branch people we tangled with earlier in London. This does not make sense since we heard from our people in the Palace that the bomb had killed them. I am suspicious that our people may have been captured and someone else is communicating on their behalf. I will have to be careful!

These are all set backs but having come this far I am determined to see it through. We have at least two more opportunities to succeed. If the next attempt fails, I will take personnel charge.

Chapter 9

Early next Morning, certainly before her Majesty had completed her toilet, Sir Henry Ponsonby was busy talking to officials and the British Ambassador to smooth over the evenings activities. The shooting, thanks to the fireworks, had not been heard ashore and the fighting on the dockside was put down to sailors' high spirits. The exploding torpedo boat was harder to gloss over, but after much expounding, everyone seemed satisfied with the explanation that a faulty boiler valve caused the ships boiler to blow up. The remains of the dead men were collected aboard the other British Naval vessels along with Lieutenant Scott-Hamilton, who we claimed had also been on board the torpedo boat. The will be transported back to England for identification and burial. It was decided that Mr. Scott-Hamilton would not be replaced since his Colour Sergeant had performed so well and as a result Her Majesty granted him the local rank of Lieutenant for the remainder of the operation. I made a note that if he continued to work as well as he did we would get him transferred to the Special Branch.

During the morning we had Mr. Parsons' boat lifted out of the water and onto the specially designed rail flat attached to our train. It was then securely covered in tarpaulins to stop prying eyes. As an after thought, we remounted the deck gun on the observation deck on the rear most carriage. It also was covered in a tarpaulin.

After a small but gracious ceremony on the pier, with Her Majesty accommodated in a beautiful red velvet and gold tent and surrounded by French Generals, she boarded her seven-carriage train and departed for Menton. The time was 10am. Again, I split our forces. This time I put Captain Singh on board the Queen's train, along with a section of guardsmen and Lancers. The Queen had specifically requested Captain Singh's presence. She had been taking Indian dialect lessons and wished to converse with Captain Singh in his native tongue. Colour Sergeant, or as he was now Lieutenant Wallis was in charge of the reaction force on our train. The sailors from Mr. Parsons' boat had adopted a parental interest in the remounted deck gun. Since they were used to firing it from a moving platform, it seemed sensible to allow them to continue to operate it. I did not foresee any circumstances that this would be required but it was always better to be prepared.

The journey weaved its slow and sedate course across France. We never traveled faster than 35 mph during the day and 25 at night. We transited Paris during the night and stopped for a short time on the outskirts to take on coal and water and allow the Majesty to complete her toilet and dressing in comfort. In the distance we could see Montmartre silhouetted against the rising sun. During this time the Lancers mounted guard and all seemed to be in order, although the French railway engineers did seem to be fussing over the locomotive of the Royal train.

After the Royal Household indicated that Her Majesty was ready to continue her journey, we slowly led off with the Royal train following at the set interval. The net work of lines was complex and it was at one of these spider web like junctions that disaster struck. We were, as planned, preceeding the Royal train and had just crossed one junction when the rear guard of our train called out that the points had changed. The Royal train switched to another line and started to speed up. We spotted it immediately, came to a halt, and frantically reversed the train. Then, with our engineers leaping from the train, we tried to switch the points but to no avail. Just 100 yards from the junction was a signal box. Two of my men ran towards it, but as they did so, the occupants fired upon them. They dived for cover into the ditch running along side the railway line and made their way back towards us. Lieutenant Wallis quickly sized up the situation and jumped from the train. Using it as cover he led some of his men towards the box and engaged the occupants in a short but savage firefight. After a few minutes, we saw a group of men jump down from the signal box, run to some waiting horses, and gallop away. We rapidly dashed into the building and found the real signal men securely tied up. On releasing them, they ran to the levers controlling the points but it was to no avail, the assailants had smashed the machinery beyond repair.

We had a full set of rail plans on board our train, so briskly ran back and scanned them for any possible help. About 10 miles ahead were another set of points which would allow us to join the line the Royal train was on. I jumped onto the footplate and told the engineer to open the locomotive up and make all haste, speed was of the essence. He grabbed the throttle and with his fireman shoveling for all he was worth the train rapidly accelerated sending sparks from both the chimney and wheels as she rapidly increased speed. I had been told these new compound locomotives were fast, but I did not realize how fast. We rapidly accelerated until we were doing 80mph. The train was rocking from side to side and the carriages were being tossed around like a tail on a kite. In less than 10 minutes, we were breaking hard, as we reached the points. It was a matter of moments to change the points and the train to advance. We once again accelerated forward and soon we going 80mph again. We passed through woods that lined the track with overhanging boughs that nearly brushed the roofs of the coaches. Then suddenly a roar, and eerie darkness as we entered tunnel. It seemed interminable as the sparks from the exhaust flashed overhead and the smoke billowed in our faces stinging our eyes until at last fresh air and we were out into the sun once more and all the while the countryside was a mere blur as we sped along. We again reached a set of points and rejoined to main line.

Once on the main line, we started to reverse along it at a more sedate speed. The sailors uncovered their gun and we began to try to come up with a plan. We rounded a bend in the line and noticed ahead there were some horses and three horse drawn carriages on a narrow country road that went over the railway line via a stone bridge. The last of carriages was on the bridge over the railway line. Around the carriages, was a crowd of men with their backs to us looking up the railway line in the direction the Royal Train should be coming from. Several of the men had turbans. One of the men must have sensed something was wrong, because he turned around and saw us. We saw him tugging at another's arm and pointing at our approach. Several broke away from the main group, ran to one of the coaches, and got rifles out. The next thing we knew, they were firing at us from the bridge parapet. This was a big mistake on their part, because the sailors were looking for an excuse and instantly there was a crash as they fired their deck gun. The first round ploughed into the bridge collapsing it instantly and sending a mangled heap of carriage, Irishman, Sikh and horses onto the railway line below. Unfortunately, this also blocked the line. Neither the royal train nor ourselves could continue to advance on our diverging courses.

The naval gunfire had been enough for those hijackers not on the bridge; they quickly mounted the remaining carriages to make a get away. However, at this moment the sliding doors of one of our carriages opened and the magnificent and frightening sight of a troop of Lancers leap from the train. They quickly wheeled and formed an extended line trotting towards the carriages. The carriages tried to make a clear break for it, but the road turned in our direction and the Lancers were also advancing up the road blocking the escape. The Lancers broke into a canter and then a gallop their Lance tips dropping as one.

If the conspirators had stopped and surrendered at this stage, they may well have survived but they opened fire and wheeled in to a field where the carriages wheels sank in the soft mud and bogged in. The occupants leapt from the carriages and continued to fire at the lancers. One or possibly two of the horses stumbled but the remainder charged forward. It was a terrible sight to see the efficient machine of a lancer troop at work, the lances were raised once again, and the stains on their tips told their terrible tail.

Meanwhile the Royal train had stopped about one hundred yards on the other side of the now demolished bridge and horrified faces were seen leaning out of the locomotive at the carnage that had been their partners in crime. They must have decided to reverse and the train began to pull away. We could not follow because of the collapsed bridge. I ran to the gun deck, as it had been christened and asked the sailors if the could deal the locomotive a "glancing blow". If they hit it square on there was a danger that the shell would go straight through the whole train!

They grinned and simply said, "Like this?"

I had heard this had been done in Nelson's time, but then it was done on water. They carefully fired a round that appeared to be going short but in fact, what they were doing was bouncing or ricocheting the shell off the track just in front of the train. It bounced just in front of the locomotive and went through the bottom of the boiler and out through the engineer's cabin on the locomotive then flew over the Royal Train. The train stopped in a cloud of stream. Once Lt Wallis saw that, the Royal Train had stopped and that it was within our reach he leapt from the train and ordered his men to follow him and form a skirmish line. They then rapidly advanced towards the train every other man dashing forward about 20 paces then dropping to his knees in a fire position covering his fellows as they then skirmished through them and formed a line in front. They followed this procedure until they reached the now useless locomotive and took charge of the shell-shocked occupants of the said train engine.

It appeared that whilst the hijackers had managed to take over the locomotive they had not gained access to the Royal carriages. This was thanks to the sustained fire of Captain Singh's men though out the hijack attempt.

Captain Singh explained to us what had happened. At the morning's stop to take on water and coal the engineers on the train had been replaced. This was as scheduled, but what had happened was that the genuine replacements had been waylaid and replaced with the Fenian's men. There were about eight of them and this had raised Captain Singh's suspicions because he felt it a rather large crew for a steam engine! Some of these men had tried to board the Royal coaches claiming to be the next set of engineers, but Captain Singh and his ten men had denied them entry informing them that they were not authorized access and if they were replacement engineers, they could ride the footplate. This is indeed what happened. However, one of the Guardsmen's suspicions had been raised by the accent of an engineer who seemed to speak English remarkably well for a French engine driver and with a trace of an Ulster accent at that. Because of this, Captain Singh had reinforced the guard on the first coach and when they spotted some of the engineers crawling over the coal on the tender they had challenged them and been shot at for their trouble.

There then ensued a stand off. Captain Singh's men could not reach the locomotive and the men on the locomotive could not board the carriages. This was the state of affairs when we again met up with the train and our naval gunfire had put pay to the affair.

It took the morning to sort out the mess. French police and army appeared and took charge of the few surviving attackers. The French rail authorities cleared the remains of the bridge and pushed the wrecked locomotive off the line, so that our train could be coupled to that of Her Majesties. Once this was done, we once again set off for the South of France. Her Majesty seemed to be totally unperturbed by the proceedings and had enjoyed her time talking to Captain Singh.

Extracts of Correspondence

Dear Bertie

We have continued our journey to the South of France this time via the French Railway system. We have as is our custom provided our own carriages for the journey particularly since one can never trust foreign plumbing.

It is hard to believe that the driver of the train actually took the wrong turn one just cannot trust none members of the Empire to do a decent job. I had a wonderful instructive morning talking to my Sikh Equerry and we do believe our Indian is coming on well. He is a charming man and dealt very politely with some tiresome French rail employees who tried to come on board.

The very nice Engineer Colonel managed to redirect our train and actually arranged a diverting naval gunfire demonstration, which was hugely entertaining. This was combined with a display by the Sikh lancers.

All aimed at making our journey as least tedious as possible.

Victoria Regina

Chapter 10

Meanwhile Peter had not been resting on his laurels. His plan to send another urgent message via "The Times" had paid off and he had been rewarded with spotting a messenger visiting the Fenian Supporter at his lodgings. His men had managed to follow the messenger back to one of the large isolated houses overlooking Ealing Common.

This had happened early in the morning of the 14th March and he quickly arranged for a Police raid to take place that evening. This time he was not taking any risks, he brought in every armed policeman he could and they surrounded the house before charging in without warning.

There was a brief struggle but surprise was total and they managed to capture some seven individuals and a mass of paperwork, weapons and explosives.

After that, the paperwork was again sent to the Foreign Office in the hope they could decode and find out something of use. The individuals were a hard nosed bunch, who were either not going to talk without a lot of interrogation or were more scared of the retribution that would follow if they did talk.

Peter got his first break when news started coming back of our second success at thwarting their attacks on Her Majesty and the fact that the majority of the protagonists had been killed. One of the more defiant prisoners after being told of the failure, in an attempt at defiance and bravado boasted to the effect that it was not over yet! They had one more plan up their sleeves and this time the "man himself" would be in charge. This was later corroborated by the paperwork from The Foreign Office. They said the documents all pointed to resources and funds having been gathered for at least three separate attempts upon the Queen. On the bad news front, there was a note dated 14th indicating that they believed the people in the Palace had been compromised and therefore no more messages were to be sent via "The Times" or any other means until the final attempt had taken place. The "clock was ticking" the message said.

Despite all his efforts, Peter could gleam no more from the seven prisoners and therefore sent a telegram to me saying he believed the Jeremiah O'Donovan Rossa was loose somewhere in France and was planning one final attack on the Queen. He was convinced a detailed plan and schedule for the attack had been worked out. Also that there appeared to be no means of communicating with Rossa by his friends to dissuade him. I was therefore to keep my guard up.

The remainder of the train trip to the South of France went without incident. The Guardsmen and Lancers knew now that they were not on a fool's errand and were up against a determined and motivated foe. At every stop or delay on our journey, the troops deployed and anyone or anything seen approaching the train was subject to the most intense inspection.

Finally, we arrived at our destination; a charming little village set in the mountains on the French Italian border and overlooking the Mediterranean Sea. The hotel "Chalet des Rosiers had recently been completed in railway architecture style, with pierced and fretted valances and balcony balustrades. It was so close to the sea that one could almost throw a stone into the Mediterranean. The Royal apartments where all on one landing and each had their own sitting room. In the harbour, there was supposed to be HMS Inflexible but she had been delayed by some two days because I had requested she call in at Chatham Royal Dockyards to pick up some special stores from the Royal School of Military Engineering that was also based there.

Once the warship arrived, the supplies were ferried ashore and placed in a large barn next to a large paddock area just about half a mile from the hotel. Now that we were at the final destination, we all settled down to a routine. Mr. Parsons boat patrolled the shoreline, both day and night and the train was kept at half an hour's notice to move.

The Guardsmen put on a ceremonial guard for the benefit of the town's people, but the real guard was always lurking in the shadows both day and night in their grey suits. The Lancers on the excuse of exercising their mounts kept up regular patrols of the hills and paths around the hotel and when the Queen took excursions out to neighbouring gardens or beauty spots, they were never far away. Neither was "Princess Beatrice," who accompanied the Queen everywhere with a fully loaded revolver secreted heaven knows where on her person.

Chapter 11

We had been in location about a week when the attack came. Her Majesty as was her custom had gone for a pony and trap ride accompanied by "Princess Beatrice" and her ladies in waiting. She would not countenance a military escort, but I ensured Captain Singh's men kept her under observation throughout her trips. On this particular day, she was visiting the splendid gardens of Dr James Henry Bennet he had laid out a magnificent garden of some 8 acres.

The Garden was about a mile away and actually in Italy, on a hillside some 300 feet above the sea. The Queen had spent several hours sketching the plants and had indicated that it was time to return to the Hotel. As Her Majesty and retinue gathered by her small carriage, she was surrounded by a group of gardeners. The head of who approached her and stated in a broad Dublin accent, that he was afraid she would not be going back to the Hotel. Her ladies tried to step in front of the men to protect her Majesty, but they were rudely pushed aside and the men quickly grabbed Her Majesty and Princess Beatrice and carried them both to the Fern Grotto, where to the ladies surprise a large Balloon was tethered. The Queen and Princess Beatrice were bundled into the basket and the balloon cast off.

At that time of the day there was a very strong wind coming in from the sea, the ground having heated up and drawing the cooler air in from the sea. The balloon rose rapidly into the sky and was carried by the wind inland towards the mountains.

The Lancers observed this from their vantage point and sent a galloper to us at the hotel to alert us of the abduction. At the same time, they attempted to follow the balloon's progress but were impeded by the rough terrain and lack of roads or paths.

On receiving the terrible news, I quickly mounted a horse and along with Captain Singh, Lt Wallis and some 10 Guardsmen and Lancers galloped to the Barn where we had taken the crates from the Warship.

Over the last 10 years, the Royal Engineers had been carrying out some top-secret research in Aldershot. They had in existence a balloon and kite section designed for artillery spotting. They had been taking this a step further by developing an airship that could actually power it self. Experiments had in the past been carried out by others with steam power but this had proven too heavy. The Royal Engineers had developed an airship powered by an electric motor and a bank of electric battery cells. It was still top secret and the range was limited. However, we had it and it should enable us to follow the balloon.

We reached the warehouse where the airship had been assembled and inflated. Its sausage like silk envelope was filled with some 18-gas cells. Under this was suspended a lightweight basket with an electric motor coupled to a large propeller at the rear. Behind the propeller was a kind of rudder controlled by the Captain of the vessel. This rudder allowed the airship to go left or right and up and down.

Under the floor of the basket were row upon row of batteries all coupled to the motor via a variable resistance apparatus controlled by a lever like throttle.

The Captain of the vessel stood along side the basket, with her hands on her hips. She was wearing jodphurs, high fur lined boots, and on her head, she had a leather helmet that covered her ears and was lined with fur. On top of this, she had a pair of goggles that were pulled up and resting on the front of her helmet. Pocking from under the helmet was shoulder length blond hair, although I thought I saw a swatch of the hair was died blue! She had clear blue eyes and a ready smile.

Miss Robin Harris was the daughter of the inventor of the airship and because of her natural adventurous spirit and undoubted skill as well as her light stature had been in charge of the entire test flight program for the craft. She was one of the leading aviators in the world.

I quickly explained the situation to her and she rapidly looked at all of us and explained "If we are to have any chance of success we must have the minimum number on board. I can take you Colonel and your three lightest men. Jump to it!"

This ruled out both Captain Singh and Lt Wallis but we nominated the three lightest and jumped aboard.

Miss Robin became all business; she told us where to stand and to hang on. Then ordered the ground crew of sailors to let go of the lines. She dumped some sand over the side and then moving levers powering the electric motor. We lifted into the sky and were already going swiftly across the countryside. We could see the shadow of the craft passing across the countryside. The motor was totally silent so all we could hear was the wind in the rigging.

We could see the balloon ahead and Miss Robin dumped more sand so that we were above it and effectively invisible to those in the basket slung below the envelope. She turned to me and asked.

"I can get you to the balloon but what is your plan? You cannot risk shooting the balloon down. One, the gas is highly inflammable so might catch fire and send the Queen to her death and two, even if it doesn't catch fire you may cause it to plummet to the ground and kill the Queen anyway."

I was training my binoculars on the balloon and had noticed a line running from the basket to the top of the balloon. I asked Miss Robin what it was for.

"Oh that, that is for regulating the release of the gas so that you can control the decent." She said.

If someone could get onto the top of the balloon could they release the gas slowly?" I asked.

"Yes." she said, "But rather you than me!"

On board our airship, we had a rope ladder, which we could lower over the side. This we did and as we silently approached, the balloon from above I stepped out of the basket and proceeded to climb down the ladder standing on the lowest rung. One of the soldiers leant out of the basket and gave Miss Robin final directions as we approached the balloon.

The balloon's envelope was made of silk and it was contained in a kind of large cargo net. I steeled myself and when my feet were practically touching the balloon, I stepped off and grabbed the cargo net. I was lying flat on top of the balloon and my additional weight had resulted in the balloon sinking. We quickly rose again I assume this was because the pilot must have thought he had hit an air pocket and dumped some sand.

Holding grimly onto the net, I maneuvered myself to the valve. I then pulled the rope, which opened the valve, and the gas started to escape. The balloon began to sink, and then rise, then sink, as the battle between dumping of ballast and gas continued. The balloon was beginning to loose its shape and we were sinking rapidly. I shut off the valve because I was afraid of injuring the Queen. Miss Robin came in again and I managed to grab the ladder and was pulled off. This slowed the rate of descent but by now, there was not enough gas remaining in the envelope to keep the balloon aloft.

I could now see we were over some very scrubby areas on the top of some rolling hills. In the distance there was a race going on. From the direction of the sea, the Lancers were frantically making their way up the slope following the balloon. From inland, there was a group of horsemen being followed by a carriage again making for the eventual landfall of the balloon. Unlike the occupants of the balloon, they could see our airship and what we had been up to. Until the Lancers could get to us, we would be outnumbered. However, I had not realized that Miss Robin had a couple of tricks up her sleeve. She leant down into the basket and pulled out some rocket shaped projectiles with fins on the back.

"When I tell you Colonel drop these as near to those horsemen as you can," She shouted. I nodded that I would try.

She turned to her controls and pulled a lever which sent the airship into a turn, and it rapidly began to advance on the horsemen. She shouted, "Now" and I dropped the first one. It had a kind of whistle in the nose so made a screaming noise as it plummeted towards the ground. This unnerved the horses and they began to rear up. Then as the thing hit the ground, it exploded. Sending clods of earth into the air. This totally panicked the horses and the riders lost all control, being carried away by the horses in a headlong-uncontrolled gallop... By this time, we were turning back towards the balloon and were over the coach. I dropped the other rocket projectile and again the horrid whistle and more by luck than judgment, I hit the coach destroying it and sending the horses charging off.

Miss Robin had brought us into a very gentle landing some 50 feet from the balloon. It had not had such a gentle landing, their basket was on its side and the four occupants were sprawled on the ground. Her Majesty, Princess Beatrice and two men. One man appeared to be the pilot and was trying to hide behind the basket; the other man was pulling her Majesty to her feet and had a revolver pointing at her head. He was standing behind her facing us as the three of us approached.

He called out to us.

"I assume you must be Colonel Prendergast the man that has caused me all this trouble and thwarted all my plans!"

I called back locking eyes with him and still slowly advancing,

"I am and I assume you must be Jeremiah O'Donovan Rossa!" I looked to her Majesty, "Are you alright Your Majesty?"

"We are, thank you Colonel, but I am not amused by the conduct of this man!" Her Majesty replied

"Colonel," Rossa said, "I have nothing to loose now so unless you lower your weapons I will kill the Queen here and now!"

I had noticed some movement behind Rossa but did not want to switch my gaze because of the risk of alerting him to his impending danger. I told the Soldiers to lower their pistols and at this very moment.

Princess Beatrice spoke to Rossa

"You know, the Colonel is always telling me off for going for head shots, but I prefer them, because they are so much more instant!" Miss Nichola had the barrel of her Adams revolver well and truly screwed into his right ear and from the look on his face, it was extremely painful.

"Very carefully remove your finger from the trigger of your gun and lower your weapon to the ground!" she said in a voice that certainly did not brook disobedience.

Rossa very carefully complied and raised his hands. We dashed forward and took his and the pilots weapons and then moved to Her Majesty's side. "Your Majesty, it will take some hours to get some transport up here suitable for you to travel back in to the hotel. On the other hand, if you have not had too much of air travel may I introduce you to Miss Robin, who along with Miss Nicola, would be more than honoured to transport you back to the hotel by airship." I suggested.

Her Majesty looked at the collapsed balloon then the airship sitting proudly on the ground, with Miss Robin standing equally proudly along side it.

"We would be pleased to be conveyed by airship." She stated." If my dear Albert had been alive he would have wanted to fly."

Jeremiah was handed over to the French authorities. Now the Queen we hoped would be allowed to enjoy her holiday in peace and quiet. The real Princess Beatrice arrived by train to stay with the Queen and act as her companion, but her Majesty specifically asked for Miss Nicola and Miss Robin to stay for the remaining period of her vacation.

Extracts from correspondence

Dear Bertie

We had yet another most diverting time today. We went with our female companions to Dr Bennet's delightful gardens. They are set in the mountainside overlooking the sea, and are just a short ride in my pony, and trap.

We spent a most relaxing time sketching the flora when it was time to leave rather than take the tiresome trap back to the hotel some enthusiasts had arranged for Beatrice and ourself to take a balloon ride. I cannot say I was very taken by the experience; one is very much at the whim and mercy of the elements. In particular the getting in was most undignified and un-lady like and the landing was positively brutal.

However, that very nice Engineer Colonel came to our aid and brought a much more modern mode of air transport. This not only could be steered and controlled it was positively comfortable. Your dear Papa would have enjoyed the experience.

It would have done you some good I believe since you are not allowed to smoke on board the airship because the gas that lifts the craft is highly inflammable.

Victoria Regina

Chapter 12

It was some 10 days after the events involving the balloons that once again bad news arrived. This time not from London but from Paris. A very embarrassed Chief of Police called upon Sir Henry and shortly after, I was invited into his office.

"Please sit down Colonel, I have some unbelievable news. Rossa has escaped!" He exclaimed. "Apparently some of Rossa's men disguised themselves as police officers and casually walked into the Paris Police HQ where he was being held and rescued him. He escaped in the early hours of yesterday morning and whilst the French police seem confident they will catch him, to be honest they have no clue as to his whereabouts or his intentions. What do you think Colonel? Do you think he will run and hide, or will he try again to attack Her Majesty?"

I sat and thought for a few moments.

"I very am very much of the opinion that he will try again. Even after he knew we were waiting for him, he still tried to abduct the Queen by balloon. I think it has become a point of honour and he will definitely try again. Can you convince the Queen to leave early?" I asked.

"No, that is out of the question, she is determined to stay to the end of her vacation, as planned." Sir Harry replied.

"Very well, but can we at least convince her to go back via HMS Inflexible? That way we would at least be certain of her arriving back in England and not having to depend upon the French Railways!" I said

"I will do my best to convince her Majesty, I think that might be possible." He replied. "In the meantime do what ever you deem necessary, but remember Her Majesty will not countenance being surrounded by military guards."

"Yes Sir Henry" I replied. I went to my quarters and summoned Captain Singh and Lt Wallis. In the mean time, I also telegrammed Peter with the bad news and asked if he could find out anything from his contacts in London.

The next day Sir Henry sent a message to me, explaining that Her Majesty had graciously agreed to change her travel arrangements and return to England on board HMS Inflexible. However, she would not change any other of her arrangements. Except that is for one. It would be Princess Beatrice's Birthday on the 14th April. Her Majesty had been planning a birthday party for the Princess on board the Royal Yacht Victoria and Albert. She did not wish to hold it on board the warship, so she would hold the birthday party the last night of their stay in Menton.

Overall, it was better than I could have hoped for, although I do not think the Captain of the Inflexible agreed. At first, The Captain was totally overjoyed at the prospect of the Queen traveling on board along with her Royal household.

The reflected glory on him and his ship would give him great kudos over his fellow Captains. However, then the reality kicked in. The number cabins he was going to have to hand over to The Queen and her retinue. The decoration of these cabins to the Queen's specifications. The dinning requirements and the level of accommodations. The full realization of the implications started to dawn. The telegraph between Menton and the Admiralty fairly hummed. Each day his ship's carpenters were seen running ashore heading for the local chandler's yard and timber merchants. The Purser, was seen calling at the linen shops and local provision shops purchasing linen sheets, towels, soap and all manner of luxurious items not normally the fair of the average "tar". I did notice some sport taking place with worried officers from the ship asking members of the household's advice and being told to buy some rather outlandish pieces of equipment. The local tailors were also doing a good trade in sprucing up formal uniforms.

The time ticked by and if it had not been for the fact that Rossa was still on the loose it would have been an enjoyable time. The weather was pleasant, the accommodations were good and the company was outstanding. However, Rossa was not only on the loose, he had completely dropped out of site. Peter had been raiding every Fenian supporter's house he could find. Those in gaol were interrogated but no one seemed to know where Rossa was or what he was planning. All Peter could find out was that if Rossa wanted to get to the Queen then nothing on Heaven and Earth would stop him.

We got the French police to send us photographs of Rossa and all the soldiers were given copies so they knew what he looked like. We even had some made with different styles of facial hair drawn on so they would hopefully recognize him if he tried to get near the Queen using a disguise.

We put posters around town with his picture and offered a reward for information. We randomly changed our guard patterns and ensured the Queen was never out of our sight. We also always had a section of men at instant readiness so that they could come to Her Majesty's aid.

During this time, the Queen hosted several private dinner parties. Since most of the guests were royalty and relatives we had to be discrete about cross-examining them but with the aid of Sir Henry who knew most of the guests personally, we were able to keep security tight and inconvenience to a minimum.

We still had had no sightings of Rossa and we began to think that perhaps he had given up and gone back to America. About this time Peter sent a telegram from London he had heard from his contact in Boston. They had been following up leads in Boston and checking paper work that they had found in Rossa's lodgings. Peter had sent them the key to the coded messages we had found in London in the hope that it would work on any messages found in Boston. This hunch had paid off and some papers that had originally been dismissed as meaningless had turned out to contain some frightening news.

According to the documents Rossa, posing as an agent for the French military, had purchased two of the latest 10 barrel, 1881 model Gatling guns! These guns were point 45 caliber and could fire

1200 rounds a minute. They had been shipped along with 10,000 rounds of ammunition to a warehouse in Paris, which was purported to be a French military depot. Peter had telegrammed the British ambassador and two of his "diplomatic staff" had checked the warehouse out. It was not owned by any part of the French military, but in fact was owned by the same company that had owned the warehouse we had visited in London. The warehouse was empty and there was no trace of any Gatling guns. However on questioning some workmen who were cleaning the building did say they remembered some large crates arriving from America and then the self same crates being sent somewhere to the South of France!

Peter's agents had decided that because of the size of the crates the only practical way for them to have been transported to the South of France was by sea, by riverboat or train. They decided to concentrate on the riverboat and train options first. After a busy couple of days, going to shipping agents and rail freight offices, they finally had a stroke of luck. They found a freight clerk who remembered the containers because they had the United States of America flag printed on the side of them. He confirmed they had been sent a week ago to the freight offices in Nice. Having found this out, the agents caught the next express train to Nice. Once there, they again tried to trace the crates. They found that the boxes had arrived safely and had waited to be collected for three days. They were collected just two days ago by a group of foreigners one of whom the shipping clerk confirmed from a photograph shown to him as Rossa. The crates were taken to the harbour where they were loaded onto a coastal barge. This was where they lost the trail because the local mafia owned the barge and no one was going to cross the mafia.

On reading the telegram I immediately alerted Sir Harry to the bad news that Rossa had not given up and had been seen in Nice just two days ago. I then gathered Capt Singh, Lieutenant Wallis, Mr. Parsons, Miss Nicola, and Miss Robin and told them of the situation. We tried to envisage what Rossa had in mind and what he would do. We also tried to think of ways we could counter the threat. One thing was obvious it was pointless for Miss Nicola to take the role of

Princess Beatrice since Rossa could now identify her.

We came up with several schemes we thought Rossa might try, but felt our security measures effectively prevented them. The only thing we could come up with was that we should all be on high alert, the airship, train and boat should all be ready to go at a moment's notice. I also asked Lieutenant Wallis to get his best riflemen to get out their rifles and start practicing their long-range skills. I had John Brown, Her Majesty's personal servant and himself an outstanding rifle shot, to fit the best two riflemen's rifles with telescopic sights from the royal armoury.

Chapter 13

The end of the Queen's sojourn in the South of France finally was arriving and along with it Rossa's opportunities to strike against her. As each social engagement came and went, our level of nervous expectation grew, and with it our sense of overwhelming relief when the event passed without incident. The Royal Household began to pack items that were no longer required and crate them up for transportation back to Windsor. These crates were then sent down to the harbour for transfer to HMS Inflexible. My only consolation at this time was the fact that the Captain of HMS Inflexible seemed even more careworn then us.

Finally the last evening arrived and preparations were in hand for Princess Beatrice's birthday party. We doubled the guard and searched the grounds and the hotel building before the event. We checked all the guests' identities and generally tried to cover every eventuality.

The festivities began with the Band of Marines from the Warship playing a selection of music. Guests arrived and the Queen and Princess Beatrice circulated greeting guests and generally looking radiant. The kitchens, under the supervision of the Royal Chef, had produced a magnificent cake. It had twenty-five candles on the top marking Princess Beatrice's 25th Birthday. The moment came and the cake was wheeled in on a small table and placed in front of the Queen and Princess Beatrice. Behind the Queen was John Brown, resplendent in his kilt and full beard. He was a dour man, but some how he looked even more grim tonight. Rumour had it he was not a well man. Sir Harry gave a nod of his head and the servant leant forward and lit the twenty-five candles. I was on the other side of the room trying to watch everything. The servant was putting the match to the largest candle in the centre of the cake when it happened! Instead of a flame, there were sparks as if the candle was a fuse not a candle. It was in fact a fuse! There was a quick fizz and then an almightly blinding flash followed by choking smoke. We were all blinded and coughing but nonetheless I was trying to force my way through the crowd to Her Majesty.

Someone showed enough sense to open the doors and windows to clear the smoke. As the smoke cleared, we realized the Queen, Princess Beatrice and John Brown were no longer in the room. It turned out that the cake had been substituted for a copy made up of cordite and magnesium powder. I ordered a total search of the building and for Lieutenant Wallis to check the guard to find out if the Queen had been seen outside. We soon found the body of John Brown in a cupboard stripped of his kilt. Rossa had somehow got to him, knocked him out and taken his place. The chef was found along with the real cake in a store cupboard in the kitchens. Finally Lieutenant Wallis came running in to confirm his men had seen John Brown driving the Queen and Princess Beatrice out of the grounds, yelling that there had been an attempt on her life and he was taking her to the battleship for safety.

I ordered Captain Singh to mobilize his men and search the countryside. It did not take long for them to confirm the Queen had not been taken to the battleship. Later a Lancer patrol found the carriage. It had been driven to a 1700 century bastion just about half a mile from town. The Bastion was on a cliff top with commanding views all around it. Inside two of the old gun embrasures - one commanding the land approach, the other the sea approach - we could see the Gatling guns.

Having discovered this, Sir Henry, as head of the Royal Staff and Household, went with an escort to try to negotiate with Rossa. I sent Captain Singh and Lieutenant Wallis to ensure the area was completely sealed off so that Rossa could not sneak away.

I also sent a messenger to the town hall to find any plans of the bastion and bring them back to us forthwith. I then telegrammed Peter and informed him of developments. It was clear from the fact that Rossa had gone straight to the bastion and had equipped it with the guns and one suspected food supplies, that he was not worried about being trapped in the stronghold. One assumed that Rossa would try to negotiate his freedom and what ever he wanted in exchange for the Queen and Princess Beatrice. I on the other hand knew that the Queen would not allow any form of weakness as she saw it and would not agree to any form of "deal" with an enemy of the Empire.

It was now early morning and Sir Henry had returned. He explained that Rossa would not allow anyone or anything within 300 yards of the building and had fired the Gatling guns to show he was serious. His demands were quite simple; the return of the Koh-I-Noor Diamond and home rule for Ireland. He stated the diamond was to be delivered to the US Embassy in Holland. Once he had confirmation that they had it, he would release Princess Beatrice. The Queen would be released when she signed a Royal Proclamation declaring Home Rule for Ireland. Rossa had apparently had the document already drawn up and just needed her Majesty's signature and seal. Sir Harry told us that he could think of no circumstances in which that the Queen would sign. I asked him what would happen if they threatened to kill Princess Beatrice in front of her. He went silent and just looked at me.

He took a deep breath and stated. "Up to this moment I had not realized what a ruthless man you had been chasing. What do you suggest?" he asked.

I replied that, "At this time I was not certain but I need time to plan, you must buy us some time by continuing to negotiate."

The plans for the Bastion proved disappointing. There were no known secret passages or well shafts that would allow secret access to the barbican. In adventure stories there is always a hidden passage, but seemingly not in real life! The Count of Monti Cristo would turn in his grave! There were not even any secret paths up from the sea. There was only one entrance, which was the one we knew about, and it was facing inland. The situation was going to prove problematic. The bastion consisted of four levels plus the flat roof. The entrance faced inland and was protected by a dry ditch spanned by a wooden bridge. A spiral stairs running in a small garderobe like tower on the inland side connected the different levels. I studied the map of the area and the sea charts. I also checked the phase of the moon. It was just past full moon so the nights were generally bright depending on cloud cover with the moon being in a waxing gibbous phase. Given all these facts and data I began to formulate what I thought was a workable but never the less desperate strategy. I called for a conference of my team. All were somber and somewhat chaste for letting her Majesty be kidnapped from right under our eyes especially as we were expecting such an attack. I could tell they were all determined to regain their "names' and were willing to give their collective all in any rescue attempt.

My plan was simple in concept but complex in execution and much demanded upon the skills of individuals. The bastion was at the top of the 300-foot cliff. Not right on the edge otherwise it would have fallen into the sea years ago. This meant there was an area at the base of the cliff that could not be seen from the tower.

"Could you Mr. Parsons," I asked, "Navigate these waters at night keeping in the dead area and get to the foot of the cliff. I know the currents are strong."

Mr. Parsons stood and studied the sea chart and the tide charts after a few moments he said.

"It will not be easy but with the power my boat has I think I should be able to. How are you going to hide the smell of my smoke?"

"I thought we would relocate HMS Inflexible to be opposite the bastion that should create enough smoke to hide yours!" I answered.

"In that case, I think we can do it." Mr. Parsons stated.

"Good! Captain Singh you and your men come from the mountains of India. Are there any of your men that you think can scale those cliffs in the dark?" I asked.

Captain Singh did not hesitate, "Yes Sir I should think they all can!"

"I need two men to climb the cliff at night, silently and with out light." I proposed.

"Miss Robin, do you think you could come in at night at a great height and hold station above the tower so that some men can slip down ropes onto the top of the Bastion?" I quizzed the balloonist.

I think so, how many men do you need?

"Five plus me. " I said.

"That should not be a problem." She replied.

"Lieutenant Wallis could your sharpshooters ensure that they shoot anyone who tries to fire the Gatling gun?" I asked.

"Not at night sir. We could not see them." He replied.

I thought for a moment then said. "If you saw them fire the gun during the day you would know where they stood to turn the crank. Then if they, the sharpshooters, peg a line pointing at that location couldn't they blanket that area with shots?"

"Yes sir I think they could it but it would need a lot of practice." Lieutenant Wallis stated.

"Well get them practicing." I said.

Having all agreed that the basic skills were present to carry out the rescue we left a guard force to keep Rossa contained and went to an area that we could practice our plan. About two miles the other side of Menton was an old Martello tower that was ideal for the purpose.

During the day Sir Harry spent most of his time sending telegrams to the Prime Minster and then trying to talk to Rossa. Most was to little effect although he did manage to get Rossa to bring The Queen and Princess Beatrice to the roof of the building to prove they were alive and well. Princess Beatrice called down to this effect.

Also during the day Lieutenant Wallis arranged for some of his men to stray too close to the tower and as a result the Gatling guns opened fire. They did not hit the men but it gave Lieutenant Wallis the information he required. He had three men with prismatic compasses taking bearings on the embrasures and another three measuring the angle up from the sharpshooters hide to the Gatling gun gunners. With this information, he could pin point the position of the gunners in absolute darkness.

It was decided that we would attack just before dawn. Captain Singh thought it would take three hours to scale the cliff; he had nominated himself as the lead climber. Mr. Parsons felt for his part it would take about three hours to creep around the headland. This set the hour to start at 11pm. During the day HMS Inflexible had repositioned and was now anchored facing the tower. At our request the battleship was still producing copious amounts of smoke that was drifting ashore around the tower.

We wished Mr. Parsons and Captain Singh well as they set off. The rest of us then went about our set tasks.

Mr. Parsons, despite having probably the most powerful boat of its size in the world and being an outstanding sailor, nearly rammed the boat into the cliffs innumerable times and on others was forced to use full power to keep the boat being dragged out to sea and into view of the bastion. The currents and tide were incredibly powerful and it was a true wrecking coastline. After a considerable time an exhausted Mr. Parsons got the boat, minus several layers of paint, into position and having placed some large rope fenders around the sides of his vessel, held it firmly against the cliff so that Captain Singh could scale the cliffs.

Captain Singh stood on the deck of the boat and looked up at the cliffs. They were vertical and the rock fractured from sea and frost action. As he started to climb, he found that at first, it was not too difficult; they just had to be aware of the slippery surfaces of slime and seaweed. However as they got higher, the condition of the rock got progressively worse. Each time they put a hand or foot on a rock it splintered and broke off. In addition, the cliff was the nesting ground of a colony of sea gulls; these screeched and dive-bombed the climbers as they struggled through the cliff face colony. They had to protect their eyes and noses from the savage pecking of the outraged parents of yet to hatch eggs. Both climbers pulled behind him a thin line that would pull up a thicker cable. Mr. Parsons and his crew were feeding the cords out extremely carefully. This was so that a sudden swell or trough did not course the lines to be snagged, or worse to pull the unfortunate climber off the rock face to his certain death on the rocks below. Some three hours of narrow escapes later, the two climbers with bloody hands, feet and knees, and guano-encrusted heads arrived at the top of the cliff. They silently lay at the foot of the tower and tried to recover their strength. After about half, an hour Captain Singh felt they were up to the next task of dragging up the cliff face the large cable that was vital to the plan.

Meanwhile Lieutenant Wallis and his men were positioned around the tower ready, if all else failed, to charge the tower and take the gate by force. Wallis also had his sharpshooters lined up to fire on fix lines into the gun ports that had the Gatling guns. The sharpshooters' rifles had been mounted on boards and sandbagged in position so that the every shot would be as true as possible.

Five men and I were with Miss Robin. We were going to abseil onto the roof of the building an hour before dawn and attempt to secure the Queen and Princess Beatrice. We would then, with the aid of Captain Singh and his man, effect their escape before the garrison of the tower knew what was going on.

At 4am, we boarded the airship and Miss Robin carefully and skillfully piloted the airship high in the sky. She kept in a cloudbank as she edged over the tower. I was the first over the edge and slid as fast as I dared to the tower roof. I touched the roof and sank into a crouch looking around me. Luck was with me, there was a guard on the roof, but he was leaning against the stairwell with his back towards me staring inland. I wasted little time on him coming up behind him and with my knife cutting his carotid artery. At the same covering his mouth so that he did not utter a sound. The knife was razor sharp so the blood from his artery pumped copiously out; he lost consciousness in less than a second and a half sinking to his knees with hardly a sound. As soon as it was clear, I used my lantern to signal to the others that they could descend.

We secured the roof, and then entered the stair well. The tower containing the stairs had a solid oak door which was clipped open it could be secured shut from either the roof top or from inside the stair well. We cautiously entered the spiral stairs and carefully and silently descended expecting at each turn of the stairs to come face to face with another of Rossa's men. We descended to the level just below us and I inched my head around the opening to see whom if anyone was stationed there. The level consisted of a large guardroom and a single cell like room secured by another oak door with a small barred opening at eye level. The door was held shut by a hefty padlock. In front of the door was a chair and table, sitting at the table was a quietly dozing sentry. In front of him was a pistol and sword. I signaled to the others to be quiet then with great care took aim and threw my kukri at the mans chest. The weight of the knife was such that it drove the knife straight into his chest and into his heart killing him instantly. I ran across the guardroom floor and caught his body before it slumped onto the floor. Unfortunately, the table had masked the fact that he had a bottle in his hand, which crashed to the floor. I looked at the others and indicated they should take position at the head of the stairs leading down to the next floor. The padlock securing the cell was simple and it was the work of seconds to open it.

We could hear conversation from people occupying the floor below and someone called asking if all was OK. One of my men in a passable Irish accent called back yes, all was fine and that he had just dropped his drink.

Meanwhile, I pushed the door open and inside the cell where Her Majesty and Princess Beatrice. Despite their surroundings, they both looked every inch Royalty.

"Your Majesties." I whispered, "It is Colonel Prendergast. We have come to rescue you. Have you been harmed in anyway?"

"We are perfectly fit thank you Colonel." The Queen replied. "However, I do not think I can make a speedy exit."

"Have no fear your Majesty we have that all in hand. Please allow me to assist you." I lent her majesty my arm and with Princess Beatrice taking her other arm, we helped her Majesty back up to the roof.

Unfortunately, at this stage Rossa must have decided that all was not well, because he and some others started to make their way to the stairs. My men opened fire and there started quite a firefight. We slowly retreated to the roof of the tower the whole time keeping up a sustained fire at the men below. We left the Queen in the centre of the roof and lowered a short rope over the sea edge of the tower. I felt it grabbed below and then two short tugs signaled me to pull the rope back up. Fixed to it was a more substantial cable that Captain Singh had brought up from the boat. We tied it around the base of the stair well and then I signaled HMS Inflexible, which in turn signaled Mr. Parsons who pulled away from the cliff towing the rope until it was tight. Whilst this was happening, Captain Singh and his man quickly climbed the rope to join us.

I turned to her Majesty and explained that whilst it was not fitting it was the only way down. We attached the special harness and without giving her Majesty, time to object swung her over the edge and allowed her to slide down the rope to Mr. Parsons' boat. This was all very nerve racking particularly knowing we were sending our Monarch hurtling towards the sea on the end of a rope and the only thing stopping her hitting the deck of Mr. Parsons's boat being a thin rope we were paying out behind her Majesty slowing her progress. As she approached the end of her journey, we applied more pressure slowing her down further so that she touched down gently on the deck and was escorted to safety by Mr. Parsons himself. One of his crew released the break line and we rapidly pulled it back up and repeated the process for Princess Beatrice.

Once we were certain the Queen and the Princess were safe, we started to evacuate our men. We did not use a break line but used rope slings that we had brought with us, these slings were not so fast going down the rope as the block and tackles that we had used for the Royals and the smoke from the slings spoke of the friction that was being generated on the way down. Captain Singh and I took the place of the men at the top of the stairs and we ensured all the men left us with their fully charged pistols. When every one else was clear I turned to Captain Singh who along side me first discharged his pistol down the stair well then lent his weight to mine as we tried to swing the substantial door shut. It had sat in the elements for many years and was reluctant to move, but with our combined efforts we managed to swing, it shut and secure it. We then ran to the rope and Captain Singh slide down. I then turned to the stairs. Ross and his men were making a determined effort to smash the door open I measured the distance to the rope and steeled myself. I slid down the rope and was about half way down when there was a flash followed by an explosion as Rossa blew the door off its hinges. There were some shots in my direction and then the rope went slack as Rossa's men cut the rope.

At this stage I was still about 100 feet in the air. I pointed my feet since I had no time to swing myself into a diving position. I looked up because I knew if I looked down, I would cause myself to tumble in mid air. As I fell, I heard the crack of bullets passing me thankfully being such a rapidly falling target I was a hard object to hit!

I plummeted into the water in a shower of bubbles and froth. I sank some distance and had to strike hard for the surface my nose was full of salt water and I was struggling to hold the remaining amount of my breath. The majority of it seemed to have been knocked from my body. I broke surface about 30 feet from Mr. Parsons' boat and struck out for it as quickly as I could. All around me there were little cracks and splashes as the occupants of the tower kept up their sustained fire at me. As I approached the stern of the vessel, I make certain its powerful propeller didn't cut me up into little pieces.

As soon as I was safely pulled aboard, Mr. Parsons signaled to the battleship and they signaled the shore. Sir Henry saw the signal and addressed the tower calling upon Rossa to surrender. A hail of gunfire came from the tower, which was answered, by Lieutenant Wallis's sharpshooters and a 16-inch broadside from the warship, which effectively obliterated the bastion.

"When the Queen of England was not amused she was not amused!"

We never found the body of Rossa but a couple of months later we heard he was back in the USA. We can only assume that when the battleship opened fire he dived from the top of the tower into the sea. A dive he was welcome in my opinion to make!

The Queen decided that the threat to Princess Beatrice and herself had been effectively countered and therefore she would go back to England by train. That was a relief for the Captain of HMS Inflexible although how he was now going to account for all the expense he had gone through is an other story.

On arriving back in England I approached Captain Singh and Lieutenant Wallis to join the Special Branch they both agreed and now we await our next adventure!

Historical Notes

Whilst to my knowledge there was no plot to Kill Queen Victoria on her vacation to France the broad historic facts and background are correct

Queen Victoria did go to France on holiday for the dates mentioned with the Royal Household and a British battleship was stationed in the harbour for the duration of her stay

Queen Victoria's surgeon did fall from a train and was crushed by its wheels as a result The Queen would not travel above 35 miles an hour.

There was an attempt on her life that was defeated by Eaton School boys with their umbrellas

The Special Branch had just been set up to deal with Irish extremists.

The webley revolver was just being developed.

The turbine boat and the compound steam engines were being developed

There was a airship powered by electricity actually developed by the French not the Royal Engineers

Jeremiah O'Donovan Rossa, the Irish Fenian leader along with his colleges did exist and did carry out several attacks on the British establishment. However he did not plot to kill Queen Victoria.